LONG HELD LAKE SECRETS
ELAINE L. ORR

Copyright © 2023 Elaine L. Orr

Lifelong Dreams Publishing

All rights reserved.

No part of this publication may be reproduced, distributed, or transmitted in any form or by any means, including photocopying, recording, or other electronic or mechanical methods except as permitted by U.S. copyright law.

ISBN-13: 979-8-870383-48-4

Library of Congress Preassigned Control Number: 2023916335

LONG HELD LAKE SECRETS
ELAINE L. ORR

Book 5 of the

Family History Mystery Series

*Long Held Lake Secrets is a work of fiction.
All characters and story lines are products of
the author's imagination.*

elaineorr.com

elaineorr.blogspot.com

DEDICATION

To my husband, James W. Larkin and my siblings, Dan, Wayne, and Grant Orr and Diane Orr-Fisher. And my nieces, nephews, grandnieces and grandnephews. I'm glad there are too many of you to name.
Family First.

Love,
Aunt E.

ACKNOWLEDGMENTS

Stories can come to an author, but few good ones are written without some research on the area, its history, or its inhabitants. I've grown more comfortable with the history of Garrett County, Maryland, and did get to visit Oakland and the area around it this year. However, I knew almost nothing about the creation of Deep Creek Lake, the beautiful source for power and recreation. The dam and land around it are today managed by the Maryland Department of Natural Resources.

A short video on dam construction
https://youtu.be/NKMJ0T6-XtY

Basic description of the dam today:

https://dnr.maryland.gov/pprp/Pages/DeepCreek/index.aspx

Because much of *Long Held Lake Secrets* revolves around the thousands of acres of farms and homesites submerged to create the lake, I wanted to learn about how things looked before the Youghiogheny River was dammed to form it. That was 100 years ago! As usual, the Garrett County Historical Society had information. In its virtual map room, I found a document that helped me get oriented. The county museums website is a treasure trove. As are its staff.

https://garrettcountymuseums.com/virtual-map-room/

GARRETT COUNTY MUSEUMS.COM

Look for the County Road Map, Youghiogheny Hydro-

Electric Corporation

1924 Map of roads to be relocated for flooding of Deep Creek Lake

Dimsey's Domain calls itself the online attic for Chris Nichols, and they have a terrific map of Deep Creek Lake – Then and Now. The base layer is the 1901 topographical and election district map when it was just Deep Creek, not Deep Creek Lake. They then laid over bathymetry [depth of water] and sonar imagery of the lake bed, along with current-day roads, property developments and other modern features. Cool to look at or buy.

DIMESY.COM

https://dimesy.com/deep-creek-lake-then-and-now-map/

Realtors in the area have written lots of history. Not to make other realtors angry, but Taylor-Made Deep Creek Sales has beautiful pictures, videos, and history articles. Chris Nichols, of Dimsey's Domain, works for them.

TAYLOR-MADE
DEEP CREEK SALES

The Jones Raid Into Garrett County, Maryland (2004) is a short booklet that brings the Civil War into Oakland, MD. The author is the late District Court Judge, Ralph M. Burnett, and it's available at the historical society.

The Policy Manual for the Maryland Natural Resource Police helped me understand how the state works with county governments relating to parkland. While my books don't focus on forensics or the details of crime solving, the website for the Garrett County Sheriff gives a sense of law enforcement in the area.

GARRETT CO.
SHERIFF DEPT.

Thanks to Thomas Vose, Director of the Ruth Enlow Library of Garrett County, and other library staff for hosting me for a book signing in May 2023. The five libraries in this rural county bring books to life for a far flung population.

As always, thanks to my critique friends, Angela Myers, J. Dave Webb, and Karen Musser Nortman. Special thanks to Amy Brantley for her proofreading skills. She caught the biggest boo-boo of my writing career.

BOOKS IN THE
FAMILY HISTORY MYSTERY SERIES

Least Trodden Ground
Unscheduled Murder Trip
Mountain Rails of Old
Gilded Path to Nowhere
Long Held Lake Secrets

Jolie Gentil Mystery Series
Appraisal for Murder
Rekindling Motives
When the Carny Comes to Town
Any Port in a Storm
Trouble on the Doorstep
Behind the Walls
Vague Images
Ground to a Halt
Holidays in Ocean Alley
The Unexpected Resolution
The Twain Does Meet (novella)
Underground in Ocean Alley
Aunt Madge in the Civil Election (an Aunt Madge story)
Sticky Fingered Books
New Lease on Death
Jolie and Scoobie High School Misadventures (prequel)

River's Edge Series — *set in rural Iowa*
Logland Series — *set in small-town Illinois*

Books are at online retailers, or ask your library or bookstore to order them — in print, large print, ebook and audio. All books have Barnes and Noble editions, which makes them easy to order from those stores.

CHAPTER ONE

Uncle Benjamin spoke vigorously. *"I tell you, something's wrong. In the twenty years after my Clara died, Thelma Zorn never invited me to her house for dinner. Why would she invite you now?"*

Digger couldn't hide a smirk. "Should we make a list of reasons she didn't ask you?"

"Respect your elders. Especially the dead ones."

"I respected you when you were alive and when you popped up on my kitchen table after your burial. I can still think of reasons Thelma might not invite you to dinner."

Uncle Benjamin harrumphed and floated into the back seat. *"I shouldn't have let you talk me into coming."*

"I didn't…" Digger stopped. Because Uncle Benjamin had to stay in his former (now her) home, the Ancestral Sanctuary, or with her, he often felt bored. No need to remind him he had invited himself.

"What exactly did she say?"

"She said she was going through some old family letters a lawyer sent her from her late brother's estate. Something I might want to see. That's all."

Digger drove halfway down Meadow Mountain and turned right from Crooked Leg Road to head to Maple Grove. The town of 2,000 came into view and Digger took a moment to enjoy the last light of the setting sun mixing with curls of smoke from a few chimneys. She loved autumn in the Maryland mountains.

She braked at a stop sign near the hardware store Uncle Benjamin owned long ago and skidded a few inches on the damp leaves dotting the road.

"You should get your brakes looked at."

No, Digger thought, I should probably get my head examined for letting you tag along. "You said you wanted to look at whatever Thelma found, but you also said you'd mind your beeswax."

Uncle Benjamin floated through the front passenger seat to sit next to Digger again. *"Her last sibling. That has to be tough."*

"To be honest, I don't know anything about her family. I guess I met her about fifteen years ago, when you dragged me to the Maple Grove Historical Society. She never mentioned…"

"I did not drag you. You couldn't wait to look for your great-grandparents in those old cemetery indexes."

Digger smiled. "Because you told me it was like solving a puzzle. When I told Thelma I didn't find a prize, she gave me a butterscotch candy."

Uncle Benjamin leaned forward to peer through the front window. *"I think her driveway is coming up. I can't see squat after dusk."*

Digger turned on her right blinker. "She's cooking baked chicken, and you always told her she should fry it. Please keep your culinary comments to yourself."

He started to respond, but Digger had turned into Thelma's driveway. She was visible, peering through the picture window that overlooked the porch of her large Craftsman bungalow. As Digger parked her Jeep near the porch steps, she thought she could see a furrowed brow under Thelma's snow-white hair.

Uncle Benjamin floated through the front passenger window, for once saying nothing.

Thelma opened her door and gestured that Digger should enter. "The chicken is just ready to come out of the oven."

"Maybe you can add more salt."

Digger never knew whether to be glad she was the only one who could hear him or wish others could so they would know what a smart aleck he could be.

DIGGER DECLINED A SECOND piece of apple pie and slid her chair back from the mahogany table Thelma's parents had bought near the turn of the last century. "If I ate like that every night, I'd have to buy a new bathroom scale. It was delicious."

No comment from Uncle Benjamin, who had wandered into the living room to examine items Thelma had spread on her coffee table. He had started snooping as soon as they arrived, but Thelma wanted to wait until after supper to show them to Digger.

"You're allowed to carry your dishes to the kitchen sink, but you can't wash them. I splurged on a dishwasher last month. First time in my life I've had one."

"I can at least load them."

Thelma stood, and appeared to steady herself lightly on the table. "No, the ads said you could put dishes with dried food in there and they'd come out clean. It's true. It's like having a maid."

Digger acquiesced and carried both of their plates and silverware to the sink. She automatically took the box of plastic wrap off a shelf near the sink, covered the leftover chicken, and placed it in the fridge.

Thelma did the same with the remains of the pie and pointed toward the living room. "Now you'll pay the price for your meal."

"You know I'm happy to help you with anything." And she was. Thelma had been one of Uncle Benjamin's closest friends and had shared some of Digger's own family secrets with her after he died. Uncle Benjamin hadn't even known much about them.

"Have a seat on the couch. I put some family letters on the coffee table, with the bill of sale from when my parents sold their farm to the Eastern Land Corporation in the mid-1920s. I just received these."

"I've read that the state licensed the land corporation to acquire the land for Deep Creek Lake." Digger slid onto the gray camelback sofa and turned to gently run her fingers over the hump in the middle of the back. "Did this belong to your parents, too?"

"No. They had one, but this is a copy from, oh the 1970s. Not a very modern look, but I like it."

Digger surveyed the displayed materials as Thelma sat next to her. "I didn't realize your family had to sell a farm so the lake could be filled."

"Before your time. Mine, too," Uncle Benjamin said.

Digger turned her head slightly to see him sitting on the top of the sofa's hump. She hated it when he didn't announce his location before he spoke.

"Yes. I wasn't born until 1945, so my family had lived in Oakland for many years by that time. But my mother often talked about her vegetable garden and their apple trees." She picked up the bill of sale. "These came from my brother Theodore's estate. It shows the family received $400 an acre, which seemed like a fortune then."

Digger had noted the bottom line on the document. Probably a good price for the time, but the family would have lost their livelihood. Thelma's parents wouldn't have been old enough to retire. Not that there would have been Social Security back then.

Thelma seemed to sense Digger's thoughts. "My father worked at the old Naylor's Hardware in Oakland for, I don't know, more than twenty years after they left their farm. He died not long after the original owner did, in the mid-sixties." She handed the bill of sale to Digger.

"Was your family bitter about having to sell?" Digger glanced at the paper as she spoke. The Zorn family had sold their land and house. Some people had moved their buildings before the land was flooded. Or maybe Thelma's parents' property had been one of those that had been bought because the roads that led to them would be flooded rather than the property itself.

"By the time I had any memories of conversations about it, they didn't seem to be. You have to remember that hydroelectric dam brought reliable power to the area. And jobs. I guess that softened the loss somewhat."

"Plus, the money doesn't look too bad," Uncle Benjamin said.

"What did bother them was that they didn't think the property was initially supposed to be part of the lake itself. My oldest brothers looked at the plans for the dam – this was many years later – and their farm was just inside the area to be flooded. I suppose my parents didn't look at the engineering drawings too closely. Who would?"

"*Me. Would've been nice to take a Sunday drive to look at the old home.*"

"That must have been disconcerting. To think a place you used to live would be at the bottom of Deep Creek Lake."

Thelma shrugged. "I think it was for my mother. Her parents built it. From the pictures, you can tell it was in good condition to live there, but folks they talked to about moving the house said they couldn't guarantee it could be relocated without a lot of damage."

"Ah. That would be hard to hear."

"That old house is part of why I asked you over tonight." Thelma picked up an inch-high stack of handwritten letters and began to shuffle through them.

Uncle Benjamin moved to sit between Digger and Thelma. Digger could never make him understand how creepy it was when he squeezed into a space that wouldn't fit a living person. A solid, as Uncle Benjamin had begun to refer to the living. He adjusted the red cardigan he'd been buried in and peered at the letters as Thelma sifted through them.

"I dove into those letters to read them, but it's harder than with a book because they aren't bound."

This particular skill had been useful in the past. Uncle Benjamin could search a thick tome much faster than Digger could read through it.

Thelma glanced at Digger. "My brother Theodore inherited these from our older sister, Therese. She died four years ago, and he passed a few months ago."

"I'm sorry," Digger said.

Thelma shrugged. "At my age, you expect to lose people. I won't pretend it's easy, but it's how it is. When Theodore and I talked on the phone, several times he said he wanted to come from California to bring what he called, 'a bunch of papers and stuff' to me. But then he got sick…" her voice trailed off.

"A three-thousand-mile trip is a lot harder when you're an old geezer," Uncle Benjamin said. *"Ask her how old Theodore was."*

Digger gestured to the table. "I'm sorry you didn't get to go through these with him. Was he too old to travel?"

"He was only eighty, but I didn't realize he had prostate cancer until just before he died. The lawyer handling his estate said Theodore's doctor said it generally progressed slowly in people his age, so he didn't have to do radiation or whatever." She cleared her throat. "Apparently that's only true most of the time."

"Gosh, I'm so sorry." Digger wondered how much more she didn't know about Thelma.

Thelma sat up straighter. "We talked a few times when he still could. Once for more than an hour. He said his lawyer would send me anything that had family memories, or important papers. I said fine, but I couldn't imagine what he had."

Uncle Benjamin had paid close attention to her. *"I wish I'd have been here to help her deal with this."*

In the awkward moment, Digger asked, "When did you move from Oakland to Maple Grove?"

"I got my teaching certificate at what used to be Frostburg State Teachers College in 1966, and there was an opening at the elementary school here. I thought I would just stay a year or two, but I fell in love with Maple Grove."

"It's easy to do." Digger nodded to a card table in the corner. "Did your brother's attorney send those two photo albums, too?"

"Yes. I went through them quickly. I became engrossed in these letters. They're mostly between my second-oldest brother, Thomas, and my sister Therese. He was born in 1925, so he heard a lot about the farm my parents had to sell."

Digger said the names silently. Theodore, Thelma, Thomas, and Therese.

Uncle Benjamin rose from the couch. *"What were the parents thinking? That's way too many names that start with the same letters."*

"So, there were four of you?" Digger asked.

"Five. My brother Thad, Thaddeus, was killed in 1945, in Germany. Just when my parents had begun to hope he would make it home." She smiled, sadly. "I was born a few days after they got word. My mother said it brought at least some joy."

Uncle Benjamin turned his head, sharply, toward Thelma. *"She never told me that."*

"So, you were the baby?"

She nodded. "My mother had children between 1920 and 1945. Not as uncommon then as it would be now." She handed one of the letters to Digger. "Read this, if you would. It's from Therese to Thomas."

Digger took the letter as Thelma said, "Thomas was born in 1925 and Therese in 1930. Thaddeus, the one who died in the War, was born in 1920, and Theodore was only seven years older than I am. He was born in 1938."

"Sounds like Thelma was a surprise."

Digger had to agree with him. She turned her attention to the letter from Therese to Thomas. She had used a fountain pen on the onionskin paper, so the precise writing was only on one side.

Dear Thomas,

If what you say is true, that's a fantastic story. It does sound more like a story than fact. If mother and father had gold and silver coins, why on earth would they have been buried behind some of the stones in the foundation? And why wouldn't they have dug them out before they had to leave?

We always had food to eat, but you would remember better than me that they talked about some lean years after they moved to town.

It's almost time to plant my garden. Eastern Ohio isn't as mountainous as Garrett County, but it's much cooler in the spring than where you are in Kansas. You should come to visit soon. We aren't getting any younger, you know.

Love,

Therese

Digger looked at the date on the letter. May 15, 1992. She glanced at Thelma. "So, Therese would have been sixty-two and Thomas sixty-seven. Not so old. Did you ever hear anything about gold or silver coins?"

Thelma shook her head. "Like a lot of families back then, my parents had a few silver dollars from the late 1890s and early 20th century, but they weren't worth more than a few dollars each. They kept them in a rose-colored Depression glass bowl in the china cabinet and let us look at them now and again."

"They'd be worth more now, I suppose," Digger said.

"I wouldn't mind having them now, that's for sure," Thelma said.

"Where's the letter her brother wrote to the sister?" Uncle Benjamin asked.

Digger repeated his question.

Thelma took a letter from the top of the pile. "It's here. Or I think it is. I'm not sure where Theodore kept it, or maybe it was Therese, but you can see how faded the writing is. He seemed to press firmly with his pen at the beginning of sentences, but then maybe he didn't have a lot of strength in his hand to keep pressing hard."

Digger took the letter and held it up to the lamp on her right. Uncle Benjamin moved closer and almost put his head on the paper, which annoyed Digger, though she couldn't tell him that with Thelma nearby.

Unlike his sister, Thomas had used more traditional note paper, so the ink had not been absorbed as much as with the onion skin paper. "I see what you mean." She could make out some words.

"Mother told me this not long…"

"I know she talked most to…"

"I didn't believe…"

"She did talk about…specific…near the west…"

Digger lowered the letter and looked at Thelma. "Holly and I have a really good scanner in our office. I might be able to scan this and use some photo editing software to bring up more of the faded text."

"I always knew that graphics design business of yours would come in handy."

"That would be good but, well, I don't want to lose any of these letters." She gestured to the pile.

"If you want, you could bring it to our office. You know where it is, across from the children's clothing store."

Thelma raised her eyebrows. "But you're on the second floor."

Digger and Holly had briefly wondered if they should situate their office in a building without an elevator, but few of the older

Maple Grove buildings had one. They decided they would go to their customers if someone couldn't hike the staircase.

"Yes, sorry about that. You could drive up and I could come down to get the letter from you."

Thelma's hesitation vanished. "I'm volunteering at the historical society tomorrow. I could drop it off on the way there, and you could bring it over to me when you're done."

Digger forced a smile. Her partner wasn't always pleased when she brought her history hobby to the office. Holly maintained that often when Digger dug into the past, something unpleasant popped up.

CHAPTER TWO

DIGGER GOT TO You Think, We Design in Maple Grove's commercial district at eight Thursday morning. She parked in front of the two-story building, one of a row of brightly painted structures housing gift shops, a children's clothing store, and a real estate office.

She'd arrived early enough to do some work on the program for a Chamber of Commerce Spring Gala before Holly arrived. They tried to divide the projects at You Think, We Design equitably, but it didn't always work out that way. This day would be a good example, with Thelma dropping off her letter for Digger to scan and try to decipher.

Bitsy had joined Digger and Uncle Benjamin in the office, and the German shepherd lay quietly in the sun that streamed in from the large picture window. Uncle Benjamin floated down from the attic and sat on Digger's computer screen. She glanced at him, went back to typing, and then pointed to her screen "Bitsy interrupts me less."

Uncle Benjamin hung his head over the monitor to read the note. "*But I have good ideas. You remember there are parade costumes in those two trunks in the building's attic?*"

"Yep."

"*You told me you couldn't get good parade pictures to put in the chamber's annual report last year. Why don't you get some people to pose wearing some of those costumes?*"

Digger stopped typing to regard him. He now wore a Union Army general's outfit, complete with three stars on the lapel. She put her eyes back to the screen. "Not a bad idea, but maybe pick something from earlier in Maryland history. What about Robert Garrett? He got a lot of the B&O Railroad financed. Without him, we might not be here."

Uncle Benjamin snapped his fingers and appeared in deerskin, with what Digger thought was a Pennsylvania long rifle. *"I'll be my ancestor, Meshach Browning, best hunter to ever live."* And he was gone.

She sometimes envied him his ability to think of an outfit and appear in it. She mostly preferred to put her brown hair in a pony tail and wear Dockers and knit sweaters. She didn't like to have to think too much about clothes.

A door opened and shut on the first floor, announcing Holly. She moved lightly up the stairs, entered the office, and stood with one hand over her mouth in a dramatic gesture of surprise. "Digger Browning, not only did you beat me here, you already have your coffee and you're working."

Bitsy woofed in agreement and rose from his spot in front of the window.

"I'm the epitome of conscientious work." Digger smiled.

Holly bent to pet the dog on the head, scratching him behind his ever-alert ears as she did so. She stood again. "Isn't that the Chamber Gala Program? I said I'd do half." She put her purse and a folder on her desk, which sat in the middle of the large office, and moved toward the coffee pot.

"I know. But I may need to take an hour later to scan and look at something Thelma Zorn got from her late brother.'

Holly poured her coffee. "He died recently?"

"Not sure of the exact date, but his estate attorney sent Thelma a bunch of papers and letters. One of the letters she most wants to read is so faded I thought I'd try to enhance it."

Uncle Benjamin poked his head through the ceiling. *"I want to get a look at that, too."*

Digger started and frowned toward him. Holly did a gimme gesture as she sat at her desk.

Digger grinned. "She's going to drive to the curb this morning so I can get it from her. Didn't want it out of her sight overnight."

"Can she climb those stairs?" Holly asked.

"I'm going down to get them. She's volunteering at the historical society and then I guess she'll pick them up when she's done."

"Ask Holly if her ornery grandmother will be at the MGHS at the same time."

Digger turned back to her work. "Is your Grandmother Audrey there today?"

"She's not on the schedule, but she thinks the Maple Grove Historical Society would wither away without her. So, I'd bet yes." She glanced at Digger's blazer. "No button?"

Digger lifted her blazer's lapel to show a two-inch round button that said, "I dig genealogy." The background was a lone headstone and shovel.

"Perfect. You should wear it on the outside."

"After I visit any clients we may have today. Not everybody likes my humor."

Holly turned to her computer. "They should get a life."

Uncle Benjamin almost stuck his nose on Digger's computer screen. *"Does that say The Chamber is giving O'Bannon an award? Goes to show if you hang around long enough, somebody'll give you a medal or something."*

Digger reminded herself his head wasn't really in her face. "Doug's done a lot for the chamber through the years."

Holly looked up. "Is Doug O'Bannon getting the Lifetime Achievement Award?"

Digger swore to herself. She usually remembered to type an answer for Uncle Benjamin rather than saying it out loud. "Yep. He lived not far from me when I had that house in town."

"That house with the leaking pipes."

Digger typed, "Go away."

He did.

She had just closed the Gala Program and told Holly to have a look at what she'd done so far when a horn honked from the street below. "I bet that's Thelma. Be right back."

As she got to the office door, Bitsy raised her head. "Stay with Holly, I'll be right back."

She clattered down the creaky steps and out the front door, waving as Thelma put down her car's passenger side window.

"Good morning, Digger." Thelma turned off the Ford Taurus' engine and leaned across the front seat. She thrust a three-inch pile of aged correspondence through the window. "Would it take a long time to do all of these? We've been scanning letters and such at the historical society so we have those digital copy things."

"Ha! Now you're in for it!" Uncle Benjamin swooped across the hood of Thelma's car and peered through the driver's side window. *"She's wearing that red-white-and-blue scarf I gave her for her birthday one year."*

Digger forced a smile. "I can, Thelma, but not all today, probably. Workday, and all that."

"Of course. I guess you can keep the ones you don't get done and I can get them tomorrow. Or could you drop them by?"

If it had been anyone else, Digger would say they had a lot of nerve. But Thelma had spent hundreds of hours helping people preserve local and family history. She supposed she should be gracious about it. "Why don't you honk this afternoon and I'll return what I've done. When I've finished all of them, I'll give you a flash drive with the scanned versions."

Thelma smiled broadly. "You're so good, Digger." She put up the passenger window.

Uncle Benjamin stood next to Digger as Thelma pulled away. *"Did you notice she was occasionally somewhat off-balance last night?"* he asked.

"What?"

He tapped his head with a forefinger. *"She was trying to hide it. Old people can be crafty."*

DIGGER STUDIED the letter. She had scanned it on a dark setting and then used some tools in Photoshop to enhance the faded penmanship. The first part of Thomas Zorn's letter to his sister Therese had become very clear. Digger had begun to think that it had been protected by the envelope and much of the rest of the letter had been exposed, as if someone left it on a desk or even in a drawer for a long time.

Dear Therese,

You're right, I shouldn't have left you hanging. We aren't getting any younger, but I'm not ready to head out to pasture yet. Besides, I wanted to talk to you more about it.

I know you poo-poo'd the idea of anything valuable being left in Mom and Dad's house when they moved out. But I've begun to believe it could be.

Then the text became faded and only some could be read, even after Digger's efforts.

Mother told me not long before she died that when they moved to the house in Oakland [unreadable] missing the sapphire [unreadable] ring she had inherited from her mother. She searched [unreadable].

"I know she talked most to [unreadable] in [unreadable]. Before he left, he told me he had dived [two inches unreadable] her feel better. When he told her that was why, it made her mad!

"Later he told me more, but I wasn't sure [unreadable] I should repeat it.

Then the text became more readable again, perhaps having been in the envelope instead of exposed to the air.

"Mother did talk to Thad about [unreadable] near the west wall, which is where mother kept the fruit and vegetables she canned. Mother mentioned the rosebush Dad gave her one year, and said she had him plant it near where he hid things. But on the outside of the house, of course.

I can believe Dad wanting to hide valuables in little tin boxes, but not that he would take mother's jewelry and put it somewhere just before they moved.

Do you think there could be anything to it? And even if there could be, what would we do at this point?

Give it some thought and write me back. But soon, not your usual two months, okay?

Love,

Thomas

Digger stared at the page. She might get more, but for now this would have to do. It sounded as if Thomas had talked to oldest son Thad about coins buried in the foundation of the family farmhouse. The "before he left" reference could mean World War II, and the phrase before that could have been "rest in peace." Or not.

She sat back in her desk chair and stared at the computer screen from a distance.

"Anything interesting in the letters?" Holly asked.

"Because you won't mention it to Audrey," Digger smiled at Holly, "I'll tell you her brother seemed to think their father buried some things near the foundation of the home that her parents owned before the lake flooded their property." She elaborated on Thelma's interest and that the family had sold the property but didn't initially think their house would be submerged.

"Hmm," Holly said. "You read about the land being flooded and all the trees they cut down so they wouldn't be in the lake. Seems if Thelma's family had trees cut down on their property that would be a clue."

"Good point. I'll find a way to ask her, but she may not know. She wasn't born until 1945."

"Of course," Holly said. "But even if her father buried something, that was almost 100 years ago. Seems like the water could have worn away soil that covered anything."

"Makes sense." Digger turned toward the scanner she had placed next to her computer. "I'm going to quickly scan a bunch more of these, but not read them. That way I'll be done with it."

Uncle Benjamin peered into the scanner, probably to try to read the next letter, which Digger had already placed on the glass. *"This is way too interesting to ignore."*

"Aren't you having lunch with Marty?" Holly asked. "See what he thinks about buried treasure."

Digger grinned. "I'll have to think about that. I don't want him letting on to Thelma that I've talked to him."

"Reporters do have a hard time keeping their mouths shut."

Digger typed, "So do you."

THE MAPLE GROVE CAFÉ bustled when Digger walked in at lunchtime on Thursday. She glanced at the tables scattered throughout and booths along the walls before spotting Marty Hofstedder. He met her eyes and raised a hand in her direction.

Digger nodded, headed toward him, and slid into his booth. "You don't usually beat me here."

"Slow morning, busy afternoon. I ordered you a BLT, since that's what you usually get here."

Digger had just taken the menu from its metal stand at the side of the tabletop. She slid it back. "What's going on this afternoon?"

"Going down to the Department of Natural Resources office at Deep Creek Lake. Some guys got cited last night because they were scuba diving about midnight."

"You can't swim after dark. Wait, scuba diving, not snorkeling?" Digger asked.

"Or even take a boat out after dusk. They had to have one to get to a spot deep enough to use their equipment. The citation I saw online was for scuba diving."

"Every year at least a few people try to head out after dark, but it's usually kayakers near the shore, since being in the middle of the lake is pretty obvious."

"And loud. Any sound travels on the lake."

The server arrived with their plates. "Did you guys want anything besides water to drink?"

Marty pointed toward the kitchen. "When the bigshots raised the price of iced tea to three dollars, I switched to water."

The tanned, college-age woman lowered her voice. "A lot of people did. Smaller checks, lower tips." She turned to leave them.

"I'll try to leave a good tip," Marty said.

She grinned and continued walking away. She hadn't waited for Digger's response, because Digger always drank ice water.

Marty leaned closer to Digger. "Is he with you?"

"He walked over with me, but he's sitting on the bench outside heckling anyone he knows."

"Or used to know."

Digger nodded as she took a bite. "He doesn't see it that way." She chewed for a moment. "I wish I knew how he'll do, you know, after all of us are gone."

"Morbid thought." Marty paused with his ham and turkey sub halfway to his mouth. "I never thought about it. We know he's here, or you do, and I believe you, but maybe there are lots of ghosts wandering around town."

"I don't…think so. He's only seen a couple since he's been hanging around. And they weren't people he knew in life. Seems if there were other Maple Grove ghosts…"

From behind her, a man called, "Digger Browning talking about ghosts. Seen any good ones lately?"

She looked into the smiling eyes of her high school classmate, Cameron Boyle, who clutched a bill as he headed to the cash register. "I've been reading some articles at the historical society. Maybe some of your ancestors are walking around town."

He nodded to Marty and then laughed in Digger's direction. "Don't see much of you since you moved out to your uncle's old place. Kind of big for you, isn't it?"

"My cousin Franklin built a small apartment in the attic, so he comes up once or twice a month. Uncle Benjamin's cat guards the place for me."

Cameron tapped his bill on the tabletop. "Call me if you bust any pipes." He moved away.

Digger scowled. "Not so funny plumber jokes."

"See you around," Marty said. He went back to his sub.

They ate in companionable silence for a minute. Digger broke it. "Can you keep a secret?"

"Reporters hate that."

"Okay." Digger ate a potato chip.

"You aren't going to tell me?"

"It's not my secret, and Thelma Zorn would be furious that I'm talking to you about it." She watched Marty mentally calculate whether he wanted to know enough to agree to keep quiet.

He frowned at her. "Okay. I can't imagine anything Thelma knows would be something I'd want to write about for the *Maple Grove News*."

Digger grinned. "Maybe it involves buried treasure."

He snorted and Digger described her dinner with Thelma and the letter she'd read.

"Funny if any of it's coins, since that guy last year was looking for some old ones his family had."

Digger shook her head. "Not as odd as you'd think. There weren't many ways to store wealth a hundred years ago. Unless you had some big gold nuggets or diamonds."

"Good point. Where was the house?"

"Sort of close to what's now the edge of the lake, I think near Thayerville. Her father didn't initially think it would be under water."

Marty chewed for a moment. "They bought 45,000 acres, but only flooded 8,000. I've seen a couple documents that supported initial applications to the State of Maryland for permits for the lake. Early 1920s stuff. They have a lot of information about planning and designs for the dam."

"Maybe old plat books in the courthouse would have land records that show how ownership then relates to where the lake is now."

"Maybe you should go digging, Digger."

"Sounds like the kind of work a reporter would like to do."

"Too bad your uncle can't seem to survive, or whatever he's doing, without you, or staying at his old house. He could go through some of those dusty records with me."

THELMA'S INSISTENT HONKING seemed out of character. Digger shrugged at Holly as she picked up the stack of envelopes and flash drive and started for the office door. "Must have been a long morning at the historical society."

As she stuck her head halfway into Thelma's rolled-down front window, Digger could see agitation all over the woman's face. "What's wrong Thelma?"

"Get in for a minute, Digger."

"She forgot to invite me." Uncle Benjamin floated into the back seat.

Digger felt annoyed, but complied and shut the door. "You okay?"

Thelma moved the car ahead a few feet and put it into park in the shade of a red maple tree. "I had a disturbing call this morning."

"From…?"

"I didn't even know my brother Thad had a child. Now I find out he has a great-grandchild!" She started to cry and covered her face with her hands.

Digger turned to her left and placed a hand on Thelma's shaking shoulder. "What a shock." She wanted to ask how Thelma heard this news. Her next thought was that maybe it was some sort of scam from someone who thought they could prey on an elderly woman.

"Damn. Out of the blue?" Uncle Benjamin asked.

She kept patting Thelma's shoulder as she tried to work out when the man who died during World War II would have had children. He'd been born in 1920. He could easily have been a father before he went to war, but it seemed Thelma would have heard that. Where had he served and where did he die? Thelma hadn't said.

Thelma's tears slowed. Without looking she flipped open the console between the front seats, tugged out a tissue, and blew her nose. She used the edge of the tissue to wipe her cheeks and regarded Digger through red-rimmed eyes. "I just can't believe it."

Digger placed her hands in her lap. "You, uh, had a phone call or letter this morning?"

She shook her head. "No. Well, not from the man. Sheriff Montgomery called and when I told him where I was, he came to the society." She took a deep breath. "He said he'd had a call from a German tourist, a man in his thirties, who said he was Thad's great-grandson."

"Why call the sheriff?"

"The man said he didn't want to simply appear at my door. He told Sheriff Montgomery he could check him out. Peter Becker. That's his name. The sheriff verified him."

"Sounds like something a polite young man might do." Uncle Benjamin said. *"But why now?"*

Digger shifted to look out at the front windshield again. "Has he, did he say how he found you? And why now?"

Thelma tilted her head back until it touched the headrest. "I sent my DNA to Ancestry. He said he'd loaded his more than ten years ago, hoping to find his birth great-grandfather's family."

From the back seat, Uncle Benjamin murmured, *"Uh oh."*

"I only did it because Benjamin told me it would be fun to see long-ago connections. I finally sent the DNA kit in six months ago." She blew her nose again and tossed the tissue on the floor near her feet.

"I did it several years ago. For a while a lot of people contacted me, but it's slowed down." Digger thought about one woman whose DNA test had led to her cousin Franklin's maternal ancestors. That was not such a great link.

"Were the people who got in touch with you close relatives?" Thelma asked.

"Not really. My fifth, or maybe it's sixth, great grandparents had tons of children and thus thousands of descendants. My own branch off that tree is pretty small, and I'm not interested enough to be in touch with people Ancestry tells me are fifth cousins or something."

"Of course." Thelma put her head on the steering wheel and raised it again. "I know I should be thrilled, and part of me is. But what does he want? Why now?"

Quietly, Digger said, "Would you like me to be with you when you call him?"

Thelma turned her head. "He's down in Oakland. I'd like you to be with me when I meet him later this afternoon."

CHAPTER THREE

DIGGER TOLD THELMA she had to finish something at You Think, We Design, and she'd pick her up at her house in an hour. What she really wanted to do was talk to Sheriff Montgomery.

She ran lightly to the second floor and didn't pause before opening the door to the office. Holly looked up from where she was pouring a cup of coffee. "Late for a date with Marty?"

"You won't believe this." Digger launched into a description of Thelma's call from the sheriff and her reluctant plan to meet the man claiming to be her oldest brother's great-grandson.

Holly had stopped pouring coffee, but still held the carafe in a pouring pose. "And Sheriff Montgomery went to the historical society to tell her the guy's legit?"

"I guess he thought so. I'll call him in a minute."

Holly finally put the carafe down and headed to her desk with her mug of coffee. "That'll be some big news among the senior citizen crowd."

Digger shook her head. "Thelma said you're the only person I can mention it to."

Uncle Benjamin sat on Digger's computer monitor and moped. *"It's not like I could tell anyone."*

Holly grinned briefly. "I assume Grandmother Audrey wasn't there when the sheriff came by or I'd have had a call already."

"No one else was there." She picked up the phone and dialed the sheriff's non-emergency number and was put through. She started to explain what she wanted.

Sheriff Montgomery chuckled. "I figured she'd call you."

"Did she tell you she only recently received some old family correspondence? It seems so odd that her late brother's attorney sent it and then this guy pops up."

"She didn't mention that. I got information from his passport. Don't speak German, so I called an international group of police chiefs in this country to see if the basic data was correct. They checked out where the guy was born, lives now. That sort of thing."

Digger sat in her desk chair. "And it was accurate?"

"Apparently if you know how to look it's not that hard. Seems to be above board. In terms of who he is. What he wants could be a different story. She'll have to be sure they're actually related."

"Can't you…?" Digger began.

"Gotta run, Digger." The sheriff hung up.

Digger hung up and met Holly's deep brown eyes. "I hope someone isn't trying to take advantage of Thelma."

"Maybe you better talk to her about not giving away any family heirlooms right away."

"Oh, I forgot to tell you. She asked me to drive down to Oakland this afternoon when she meets him."

Holly's eyebrows went up. "Maybe you should ask Marty to go with you guys."

"I wouldn't mind, but Thelma definitely wouldn't want a reporter…" Digger glanced at the ringing office phone. "Uh, oh. Marty. Can you get it? Then I don't have to tell a lie of omission."

Holly tossed a long, beaded braid over one shoulder. "I won't out-and-out lie."

Uncle Benjamin pointed to the door. *"Go into the hall. She can say she hasn't seen you."*

Digger almost bolted out the door and called to Holly. "You don't see me."

She sat on the top step that led to the two-story building's foyer below. She wished she'd brought Bitsy with her so he didn't bark while Holly was on the phone with Marty.

Less than a minute later, Holly called, "Come on back in."

She opened the office door and bent to pet Bitsy. "Did he believe you?"

"You might find this hard to grasp, Digger, but because most people don't generally tell fibs, their friends tend to accept what they say."

"She did a good job," Uncle Benjamin said. *"Said you planned to help Thelma with something."*

"Thanks. I'm going home to leave Bitsy and head to Thelma's place a little early. If you don't mind holding down the fort."

"Not much going on. I'll probably leave early and put the answering machine on."

Digger took Bitsy's leash off a peg by the door, which brought the happy dog to her. She clipped it on the dog's collar and Uncle Benjamin followed them down the steps. Bitsy paused to water several bushes on their way to Digger's Jeep.

BY THE TIME SHE'D put food in Bitsy's bowl and found Uncle Benjamin's cat, Ragdoll, to tell her she had chow, Digger felt apprehension rising. Even if the guy's identity was correct, he could still plan to scam Thelma. An elderly woman, the last of five siblings with no children, could seem like an easy target.

By the time she pulled into Thelma's driveway later Thursday afternoon, she had convinced herself to assume Peter Becker meant no harm. Or at least to act as if she felt that way when she met him.

A calmer Thelma slid into the front seat with a photo album and a folder Digger recognized as the one that held her family pedigree charts. "I decided to give him the kind of information he could find by doing a records search. And I'll show him some pictures of Thad and my parents."

"Sounds like a good plan."

They said little as they drove down Meadow Mountain on State Route 495, merged onto Glendale Road, and then turned south onto 219 just after driving across the Glendale Bridge as it traversed Deep Creek Lake. The blue sky, placid water, and bright orange and yellow leaves surrounding the lake seemed to have a calming effect on both of them.

"Not as many boats on the lake as usual. I suppose because it's a workday." Since he knew Digger couldn't answer him, Uncle Benjamin didn't elaborate.

They drove into Oakland and stopped in front of the Garrett County Historical Society, where Thelma had told Peter they could meet. "I bet he's a good guy," Digger said.

Thelma straightened her shoulders. "I keep reminding myself he's my great, grandnephew." She handed Digger the photo album and folder. "My hands are shaking. I'd probably drop these."

"You wouldn't want to do that." Digger beat her to the society's door and held it open for Thelma. They entered the small lobby, with light much dimmer than outside.

As Digger closed the door behind them, a man's voice called, "Aunt Thelma! You look like your pictures."

A tall, light-haired man of perhaps thirty came toward Thelma with an outstretched arm and broad smile. "I'm your great-grandnephew, Peter Becker."

The collared shirt and knotted tie under a heavy, wool sweater pegged him as someone who didn't live in Oakland. No one would dress that formally on a weekday unless they had an important business appointment. Of course, Digger thought, meeting Thelma would be important to this man.

Startled, Thelma took his hand and stammered, "My picture? Where did you see it?"

One of the local volunteers interrupted before he could answer. "We've set up a teapot for you in the staff lunchroom. You can talk more privately." He smiled and gestured down the hall.

As they walked, Thelma introduced Digger. "Her late uncle was one of my closest friends."

"A pleasure," he said.

Digger could detect only a faint accent, and couldn't discern if it was German or something else.

As they sat and Thelma reached for the teapot to serve them, Peter explained his comment. "On the Ancestry website, some of your...I guess nieces and nephews posted pictures of their parents. Some are family groups. Your sister Therese's daughter, I think it's Madeline, has a photo of you and her mother from her mother's, um, maybe 60th birthday."

Thelma had finished pouring a cup of tea and slid it across the table to Peter. "I had no idea people did that." She tapped the folder that contained pedigree charts. "I'm old-fashioned, you see. I have an Ancestry account because I wanted to load my DNA, but I've never posted a family tree or anything like that."

His brows went up, then down. "I feel lucky to have found you." His eyes went to Digger. "You are not a niece?"

She shook her head. "A friend. Thelma and my Uncle Benjamin, who died less than two years ago, were close friends. I think I was ten when I met her." She smiled at Thelma.

Peter's eyes went to the photo album on the table between him and Thelma. "Would you mind showing me pictures? I've only seen pictures online, and not many."

Thelma started with her parents and moved to her siblings.

While she did that, Digger wondered if Thelma was the first relative Peter had found. It seemed some of Thelma's nieces and nephews had submitted their DNA. Of course, they would not be as close a relative as Thelma was to Peter, and perhaps he found their trees only after learning Thelma was a match.

Thelma's siblings probably had not done theirs. Only Theodore would have been alive after the testing became somewhat commonplace. He'd never married, so he wouldn't have had kids pushing him to do it.

She glanced around the room. A huge photo of the Oakland Train Depot dominated one wall. Another of the domed county courthouse hung opposite it. From that photo, you couldn't tell that it rose above other buildings in the town that served as the Garrett County seat.

Thelma took Digger out of her head. "Do you know whether the Oakland coffee shop on 2nd Street serves sandwiches?"

She smiled. "They do. And good soup. Do you want to head over there?"

"I think so." Peter looked disappointed. It didn't appear Thelma had opened the folder of pedigree charts yet.

"She's tired," Uncle Benjamin said. *"It's hard to have a one-on-one conversation with a man she doesn't know – and about such personal topics."*

Digger had an idea. "You must be tired now, Thelma. Why don't you let Peter take photos of a couple of your pedigree charts or family group sheets? Maybe you can rest this afternoon and he could look at them this evening. You could talk again tomorrow."

Peter smiled broadly, and Thelma nodded. "I can always count on you to know the tricks people can do with those phones." She opened the folder and moved it toward Peter. "Take pictures of any of these. I'm going to the ladies' room." She smiled as she stood.

When the door shut behind her, Peter turned to Digger. "It was selfish of me to ask so many questions. I'm just so excited to meet my great-grandfather's sister."

Digger pointed to the folder. "Why don't you start taking pictures, and I might be able to answer a couple of questions for you. Not so much about her family, but where towns are, or what abbreviations mean."

For the next fifteen minutes, she helped Peter position pages for his photos, and then took her own. Thelma didn't say not to, and Digger wanted to know more about some of the people referred to in the letters Thelma had given her. She could tell Peter wondered why she was copying the pages, too, but she was not about to mention the letters.

When they finished, Peter took a photo from a manila envelope he carried. "This is my parents, and me, and my great-grandmother, Thaddeus Zorn's well…you know."

Digger studied it. "You look a lot like your own father."

He nodded. "In these pictures Aunt Thelma had, I think I look some like my great-grandfather, too."

Thelma came back into the room. She held one of the Garrett County pictorial history books and placed it on the table in front of Peter. "I live in Maple Grove, where Digger lives, but my family lived in Oakland. I grew up here. I bought you this book of pictures. When we get together again, I can show you some of the places my parents, including your Great-Grandfather Thaddeus, used to go."

For a second, Digger thought Peter was about to cry.

He recovered quickly and quelled what seemed to be an impulse to lean across the table to kiss Thelma. "I will pore over this. Can we see each other tomorrow?"

"I think so," she said. "Where are you staying?"

"The Oakland Motel. It's not so new, but the managers are very friendly. I've asked them a lot of questions about the town. They don't seem to mind answering."

"You should ask him to stay at your place. There's plenty of room," Uncle Benjamin said.

Digger shot him a look, trying to convey that she wasn't in the habit of asking strange men to stay at the Ancestral Sanctuary.

"Oh, right. Well, have Marty stay over."

She ignored him and smiled at Peter. "Why don't we head out now, and we can meet tomorrow. That okay, Thelma?" She took a business card from her pocket, wrote her personal cell number on it, and handed it to Peter.

"That sounds great," Thelma said.

Digger thought she grew more tired by the minute. She picked up Thelma's photo album and folder. "Let's walk out together."

While Thelma paused in the small reception area to thank the Garrett County volunteers for their kindness, Digger led Peter outside. As she blinked in the sunlight, a familiar male voice came from her left.

"Holly said you and Thelma had business down here today. But she didn't mention a handsome stranger." Marty Hofstedder grinned, held out a hand to Peter, and introduced himself. He nodded toward Digger. "She may not admit it, but I'm her boyfriend."

"Most days I do." She pointed to Marty. "He works for the *Maple Grove News*, where we live, up Meadow Mountain."

Peter said appropriately complimentary things about Digger and Thelma.

Marty nodded to Digger. "I came down to learn more about those knuckleheads who were trying to dive in the lake last night."

"Oh, right. Did you find out anything?"

"Not much. They aren't from here."

"*We could have guessed that*," Uncle Benjamin said.

"Like deep-sea diving?" Peter asked.

"If you can imagine that in a lake with an average depth of twenty-five feet," Marty said.

Before Digger could ask the divers' names, Thelma came out of the historical society and seemed pleased to see Marty. "Did you meet Peter?"

"I did." He didn't ask questions, but Digger could tell Marty was curious.

"Thelma and I need to head back to Maple Grove." She held a hand out to Peter. "Call or text me this evening about getting together tomorrow."

He nodded, waved lightly, and began to trudge toward the Oakland Motel. Digger hadn't thought about whether he had a car. He must. She turned to Marty. "Call me when you get home?"

"Sure." He bent and kissed Thelma lightly on the cheek, and when Digger beeped open her car's door, he opened it for Thelma and shut it when she was inside. His eyes met Digger's over the roof of the car. "Holly called. She was worried about you."

Digger nodded as she opened her car door. "I'll catch up with her later." She smiled. "Thanks for caring."

His eyes laughed. "I said Holly did."

Digger slid behind the wheel and started the car. "You okay, Thelma?"

"Basically, but I can't help but wonder at his timing. Just after I got those letters."

Digger pulled away from the curb. "I guess you have to believe in coincidences." But she usually didn't.

CHAPTER FOUR

BEFORE DROPPING THELMA at her house, Digger gave her the stack of scanned letters and the flash drive to which she'd copied them. "I was able to read much of Thomas' letter to your sister. I put a transcribed copy in the envelope with the original letter."

"Thank you."

"You can take a look at the letters. It sounds to me as if your oldest brother might have believed your father – or someone – did put some valuables near the house's foundation. Maybe in tin boxes…"

Thelma turned in her seat. "My father kept lots of small things in tin boxes. Nails, his two pairs of cufflinks. He had a tinsmith make a somewhat larger box for my mother's sewing thread and needles."

"If they weren't made well, those tin boxes could rust." Uncle Benjamin said.

"Interesting." Not really, but maybe she would think so if she wasn't tired herself. "See if you think your brother Thomas thought it could be true. It sounded as if he thinks your brother Thaddeus might have tried to find something after the house was submerged."

Thelma opened her car door, but paused before getting out. "Do you think I should show Peter the letters?"

"Maybe if some of them talk about Thaddeus."

She sighed. "None of Thomas or Therese's kids have cared a whit about family history or records. Maybe Peter would."

Digger smiled. "Hey, if you can get someone about my age to be interested, go for it."

"You're a dear. You don't mind driving me to Oakland tomorrow?"

"No problem, as long as it's not for the entire afternoon."

She watched Thelma slowly climb the porch steps to her bungalow. It seemed Peter Becker was genuinely interested in Thelma, and Digger didn't sense any hidden motives. Though how would she know?

As she drove up Meadow Mountain toward the Ancestral Sanctuary, Uncle Benjamin sat quietly in the front seat beside her. Digger glanced at him. "You aren't usually so pensive."

"I think that young man is okay, but I didn't detect a German accent. That makes me wonder."

"I didn't think to ask him anything about himself. I will tomorrow."

"If Thelma's father put items in tin boxes that have been under water, they've probably rusted away by now."

"Maybe not if they were buried and had a stone over them."

"It just seems somebody would have found something before now."

Digger smiled. "Are you saying you would have dived down to a crumbling house with an oxygen tank on your back?"

"No, but I might have talked you into it."

"I doubt it." Her mobile phone rang. Digger glanced at it in her cupholder and pushed the speaker button. "Digger Browning here."

"Marty Hofstedder here. You home yet?"

"Getting close. You want to come up?"

"You cooking?"

"I have half of a chicken and rice casserole in the freezer. I bet we can talk Uncle Benjamin into hanging out in Franklin's apartment for a good part of the evening."

"He with you?"

"Tell him he can't talk about me."

"Oh, yes."

"Hey, Benjamin. I want to pick your brain about the land acquisition for Deep Creek Lake."

Uncle Benjamin sat up straighter. *"Sure. I have some good information on that."*

Digger relayed this. Marty said he'd be there in an hour and hung up.

Digger turned to Uncle Benjamin. "I think Franklin put some of your books in boxes in that storage cabinet he built in the attic."

"Right where I want 'em. Feel free to drive faster."

AS THEY STOOD IN the kitchen Thursday evening, Marty told Digger and Uncle Benjamin where the two young men had been caught snorkeling two nights ago. "Not too far from the western edge of the lake, near an expensive tourist lodge in Thayerville. The sheriff's crime blotter doesn't mention where they live, just says no local address."

"That's not too far from where Thelma's family's farm was," Uncle Benjamin said.

"I'll tell Marty in a minute." Digger turned to Marty. "Did they say if they were looking for something in particular?"

"They said only that they were fooling around. They'd never tried to scuba dive in the dark and wanted to practice before they did a trip to the Bahamas this winter."

"Tell him about Thelma's family."

Digger pointed a finger at Uncle Benjamin. "I will if you stop asking."

Marty grinned. "I love it when you two fight. What does he want you to tell me?"

"I told you Thelma asked me to scan those letters. I haven't read them all, but the one she was most interested in seemed to imply her father buried some things near their farmhouse's foundation. It was near Thayerville, I think, and they didn't expect it to be submerged."

"Everyone knew what would end up under the lake," Marty said.

"Everyone with any brains."

"They apparently thought their house would still be standing, though there wouldn't be any roads that led directly to it. But it ended up just inside the lake. I guess fairly close to the shore now."

"Your basic lakefront property."

Digger ignored Uncle Benjamin.

"Hard to believe they didn't know," Marty said. "How fast did it fill?"

"Wait a second," Uncle Benjamin said.

Digger glanced at him and then to Marty. "He may be remembering something."

"It was supposed to take about six months to fill, but it took a lot less because of heavy mountain runoff that spring. And a lot of rain."

Digger repeated this. "It still seems like they would have had plenty of warning about the house being submerged."

Marty bent to smell the now heated casserole, which sat on the stove. "This was the 1920s and the Zorns weren't near their house anymore. Oakland seems close to us with good roads and fast cars. But they traveled on winding mountain roads. Did they even have a car?"

Digger shook her head slowly. "I can ask Thelma if she knows. But would it really have filled fast enough that they didn't know until it was done?"

"They might have found out, but the water could have risen a few feet pretty quickly," Uncle Benjamin said. *"And I believe I heard they didn't let people on their old properties as the lake was filling."*

"What did he say?" Marty asked.

Digger told him. "I suppose they could have been kept away for a time. After the house was even partially under water they would have had to dive to retrieve anything."

Marty added, "Thelma's parents probably had little kids then. Plus, they lived twelve or fifteen miles away and her father had a new job."

Digger put the casserole on two hot pads that sat on the kitchen table and began putting portions on their plates. "This was all twenty years before Thelma was born. She won't know much about her family's life then."

"You don't want to upset her," Uncle Benjamin said.

Digger nodded at him where he sat on the kitchen counter. "We don't want to upset her. It just seems odd that Peter Becker would show up just after she got those letters, and at the same time some men were trying to sneak a nighttime dive."

Marty paused with his fork halfway to his mouth. "I don't see how a couple Bahamas-bound divers and Thelma's family connect."

"And," Digger continued, "even if they did, how would divers know where to look? There are some old maps that show the area topography before and after the lake filled in the mid-1920s. But they aren't on the wall in the library."

Marty tossed a pea at her. "You've gotten hooked on solving mysteries. Maybe you can volunteer with the Sheriff Department."

"You know I don't go looking for trouble."

"Why don't you talk to your friend Maryann Montgomery?" His tone was teasing. "Her family was in Oakland, and she's older than Thelma. Maybe she remembers stories about buried treasure."

"She was born about 1930, so fifteen years older than Thelma. And you know how much Sheriff Montgomery loves it when I talk to his grandmother about anything…out of the ordinary."

Uncle Benjamin pointed toward the dining room, where Digger had her laptop. *"I want to look at those letters. Pull them up on your computer."*

"I'll open the laptop for you to look at the letters when we finish eating."

"Benjamin," Marty said. "Can't you dive into the computer the way you go into books?"

He frowned. *"I haven't learned yet. I wish I could meet a younger ghost. Maybe they'd know how to do that."*

Digger hid a smile behind her napkin. "Thwarted by technology, are we? I'll put in the flash drive of the letters I scanned in a minute. But please don't interrupt Marty and me."

Marty glanced at the point Digger faced as she talked to Uncle Benjamin. "I'm going to talk her into spending the night at my place. We might even take Bitsy, but you can keep Ragdoll."

Uncle Benjamin chuckled. *"Keep her for a week."*

Digger didn't repeat his comment, and she and Marty didn't end up setting up the letters for Uncle Benjamin to read.

FRIDAY MORNING, DIGGER, minus Uncle Benjamin, got to the office early. He didn't like being unable to offer commentary for long periods of time, and knew Digger would try to ignore him when Thelma and 'the guy from Germany' would talk among themselves. Digger left the TV on for him so he could watch Jeopardy later in the day.

As much as she loved him, it was easier not to have Uncle Benjamin around when she was talking to people other than Marty. She put the finishing touches on the Chamber of Commerce Gala program and returned two voicemails. She agreed to talk on Monday to a woman in the Maple Grove School Board office about doing a decorative attendance calendar they could distribute to parents before the holidays.

Holly came in about eight-thirty. Because her Grandmother Audrey was, as Holly said, a genealogy nut, she understood why Thelma wanted to spend time with her newly found great-grandnephew. In a mock stern voice, she added, "But I know you're dying to dig into this, too."

"I'm somewhat interested, but mostly because Thelma was pretty much Uncle Benjamin's best friend. When everyone was mad at him for insisting the historical society should move from the old Maple Grove Depot to the place in town, she wasn't annoyed with him. Or didn't show it, anyway."

DIGGER PICKED UP Thelma at 11:45 and drove toward Oakland to meet Peter Becker for lunch and more conversation about the Zorn family. Thelma again had the photo album on her lap, though she'd left the pedigree charts and such at home, since Peter had copied them.

They swung by the Oakland Motel to pick him up. The vintage 1970s motel had been well cared for, but it could not be described as plush. Like many buildings in Garrett County, it sat on the slope of a hill.

Digger pulled to the room number Peter had given them and was about to beep, but Peter came out, locked the door, waved across the parking lot to a man standing just outside the motel office, and climbed into the back seat.

"I cannot thank you enough for coming back today. The map I looked at last night showed it is almost twenty miles from Maple Grove to Oakland. Should I pay you for some petrol?"

Digger smiled. "No. When you live in a very small town you often drive to larger ones."

As she backed out of the parking lot, she saw two men sitting on a bench outside another motel room. With their sun-bleached hair and deep tans, they looked like college students trying to recreate summer, though older than that. And grungier.

Digger thought she recognized one of them, a man named Robert Thorn, who had been three or four years ahead of her in high school in Maple Grove. She only remembered his name because one of the teachers referred to him as a thorn in her side and some of the guys teased him. They stopped when he slugged another senior in the hall one day.

He was not someone she cared to know.

Thelma turned slightly to look at Peter in the back seat. "After we have a sandwich in a small café, we're going to the library. There's room to spread out, and they have a genealogy section, in case you have questions Digger and I can't answer."

They found a shady spot near the popular café. Digger would normally have deferred to Thelma to order first, but she wanted to order something simple, so lunch could be served quickly. Peter followed her lead.

He had brought the Oakland pictorial history Thelma gave him yesterday and asked her to point out where she went to high school and if her family had gone to one of the churches the book depicted. As a bonus, Thelma found a picture of the hardware store her father had worked in.

After lunch, they drove the short distance to the library and entered the brightly decorated main room. Digger stopped at the desk to tell a librarian that they would be in the genealogy area.

Thelma introduced Peter and explained that she'd grown up in Oakland and had brought a family member visiting from Germany.

The librarian smiled. "Welcome. There's a microfilm reader in the genealogy section, and it's fine if you talk quietly."

After introductions, Peter said nothing for several seconds, then turned to Digger with a wide smile. "We have a good library where I grew up, but this is a place to be," he paused, "to be part of the community."

Digger glanced around the brightly lit space, littered with books, easy chairs, and reading nooks. "I don't come here too often because we have a library in Maple Grove. But I'd have to agree with you."

Peter took a notebook and folder from his backpack and placed it on the floor under his chair. "I would really like to look at more pictures of my great-grandfather."

Thelma opened the album, but with a shake of her head. "I wish I had more. My family wasn't poor, but when my brother left for war in 1942, they didn't take lots of pictures the way people do now. I remember my mother being very upset that she didn't get back any photos he took over there."

"Perhaps," Peter studied the album for a moment, "he didn't take any."

She shook her head. "He would occasionally mail one to my parents." She turned the page and pointed to one of Thaddeus standing next to a tent, dressed in winter clothing.

Digger moved closer to see it, but his face was barely discernible. "Maybe I could scan and enlarge it, so you could see his face better."

Together, Thelma and Peter said, "That would be wonderful!" They looked at each other and laughed.

For the next few minutes, Digger feigned more interest than she felt. Thelma was very familiar with census records and showed Peter her family's names on the 1940 census. Peter wanted to know why she wasn't with her family, and appeared flustered when she told him she hadn't been born until 1945. "I forget you never met Great-Grandfather Thaddeus."

Digger stood to look over Thelma's shoulder at the census microfilm, curious about professions of the Zorn children. She realized only one or maybe two would be out of high school.

Still, she saw that Thaddeus was a clerk in a newspaper office and the second oldest, Thomas, was in school but also delivered the paper. Working with words would help explain why they wrote and kept such informative letters.

Thelma also showed him a booklet that commemorated men from Garrett County who were killed in both World Wars. Peter took a photo of the page with Thaddeus Zorn.

As they talked, Digger jotted a couple of ideas in the notebook she kept in her purse. She and Holly could ask families in Maple Grove to send pictures of service members and do a Veterans Day display. If the *Maple Grove News* would run it, it would be a form of advertising for their graphic design work.

A shadow, two actually, fell over the table where the three of them sat. Digger glanced up to see Robert Thorn and the man who had been with him on the bench at the Oakland Motel.

The shorter one, whose unshaven appearance looked more like sloppiness than planned grooming, smiled and raised one hand. But he didn't say anything.

Robert, whose blonde hair looked natural, spoke. "Hi. Peter, isn't it? We're staying a couple of doors down from you at the motel."

Peter hesitated, "Sure, but I forget your name."

"Robert. You gotta work on your memory. My buddy's Elmer. But we like him so much we call him Elmo."

Digger thought Peter looked uncomfortable. She doubted Robert Thorn would recognize her as the fourteen-year-old who'd been several years younger than he in high school. She asked, "Are you guys vacationing here?"

Elmer, a.k.a. Elmo, smiled broadly. "Kinda. Just here for a couple days."

"The water's perfect," Robert said. He didn't mention that he'd gone to high school in Maple Grove, and didn't seem to recognize Digger. He also didn't look as if he'd prospered since high school. She wondered why he'd been staying at the motel, but didn't care enough to ask.

Without saying anything else, they turned and walked toward the exit. Digger couldn't imagine why they were in the library. Had they followed Peter? Maybe they thought a German tourist would be well-to-do and wanted to wheedle some money from him.

Peter's eyes followed them, and then he shrugged at Thelma and Digger. "They want me to get beers with them. But they are a little…"

"Uncouth?" Thelma supplied.

"That is a good word."

Digger realized Peter's limited use of contractions was about the only thing that indicated English was not his first language. "Do they bother you?"

Peter shrugged. "Not really. Well, maybe some. I do not like to sit in the chair outside my door since they came."

Digger nodded to Thelma and Peter. "I don't think they mean any harm, but I can see why they'd be annoying." She stood. "My phone vibrated, and it could be business. I need to check my messages."

Digger walked past the front desk and held up her phone. "Be right back."

"Sure thing," the librarian said.

Once outside, she went to Google and put in Robert Thorn, Oakland, Maryland. Several articles from a Cumberland, Maryland paper came up. He'd been arrested on suspicion of burglary, but charges were dropped because police never found any of the stolen items in his home or car. He'd run a stop sign and broadsided a town council member's car. That got him a hefty fine.

She put her phone back in her pocket. He was hardly a responsible citizen, but he hadn't committed any serious crimes. That she knew of. Marty didn't grow up in Maple Grove, so he wouldn't know more.

Cameron came to mind, and she opened her phone again.

He answered on the second ring. "So, you miss me so much you broke some pipes at your place?"

"You're so charming. I have a memory question for you."

"Sure. What's up?"

"There was a guy a couple years older than us in high school. Did you know Robert Thorn?"

"He's a scumbag. Didn't really know him in school. He's always got some easy money idea, tries to talk people into what he calls investing."

"So, he lives in Maple Grove still?"

"Nope, but he used to bunk with his sister sometimes. Probably broke. She threw him out for good a couple years ago. I think he tried to scam some of her friends. He didn't come on to you for something, did he?"

"No, but I'm worried he might want to bother a relative of Thelma Zorn's who's visiting from Germany."

"A tourist? Jeez, that guy would be a prime target. You should warn him."

"I will. Thanks for the info."

"You're welcome. Make sure you wrap your pipes this winter. That big old house probably has plastic wrap for insulation."

Digger laughed and hung up. She moved to the shade of a tree next to the library. She liked Peter as well as you could like anyone you'd just met and didn't like the idea of Thorn and his ne'er do well pal bothering him. Should she ask him to stay at the Ancestral Sanctuary? She decided to see what Marty or Franklin thought.

Marty picked up on the second ring. "How's the family get-together going?"

"Not bad, but I'm thinking about asking Peter to stay at my place for a few days and wanted to run it by you."

Silence for several seconds, then, "Is he low on money or something? I mean, he seems like an okay guy, but you don't really know him."

"He's at the Oakland Motel. It's basic and friendly, but a couple rough-looking guys talked to him in the library just now. They're staying there, too. One was a few years ahead of me in high school. They've invited him for beer and he seems uncomfortable around them."

"Ummm."

"Tongue-tied?" She grinned. "I have to check with Franklin. He's coming up tonight. He might not like the idea."

"Sheriff Montgomery checked him out. Thelma seems to like him, right?"

"Yes, but I don't think..." Digger began.

"I wasn't suggesting he stay with her," Marty paused for several seconds. "Why don't you call Franklin? Tell him I think Peter seems okay, and I'll have dinner with you guys this evening."

"Thanks. Can you bring something for dessert?"

"Sheesh." Marty hung up.

Digger thought the call to Franklin might result in one of those are-you-sure-that's-a-good-idea conversations, but she was wrong.

Franklin got on the phone quickly because Digger rarely called him at his law office. He sounded as if he was in a hurry. "It's the kind of thing that's more common in Europe, especially among the hostel crowd, which I was part of that summer after college. Marty thinks he's okay?"

"He knows Thelma and I have been with him a lot, and he met Peter briefly. I like him."

"Sure, sounds okay. I'll be there tonight, and you said Marty's coming for dinner?"

"Yep. Should I save you anything?"

"What are you cooking?"

Digger could see him smile. He liked foods a lot spicier than she did. "Baked chicken. I have plenty."

"Sounds good. I probably won't get there until after nine."

"He'll be glad..." Digger clapped her hand over her mouth. She'd almost said Uncle Benjamin would be glad to see Franklin.

"Say what?"

"Ragdoll will be glad to see you."

"She's glad to look out that attic window. See you tonight."

Digger could feel herself flush as she leaned against the stone wall in front of the library. She and Franklin had had some awkward moments since she had told him about Uncle Benjamin's reincarnation, or whatever you called it.

She began to cool down. It would be easier to have someone new around. Fewer awkward pauses or wondering if she should tell Franklin what his father was up to, since he couldn't see him.

Marty hadn't known long, and only because Uncle Benjamin had been forced to push something off the dining room table to get his attention. Twice. Any attempt to move 'solid stuff,' as Uncle Benjamin called it, made him nearly fade away. It was not a feat he could easily repeat for Franklin.

Marty had wondered what the heck was going on with Digger. Between that and him beginning to guess Uncle Benjamin was visible to Digger, she'd told him.

Telling Marty had been hard because she'd been afraid he'd walk away. But in a way it had been easier than telling Franklin, because Uncle Benjamin wasn't Marty's father. She straightened her shoulders. She was closer to Franklin than anyone, even Marty. They'd have to figure out how to work through the awkwardness.

CHAPTER FIVE

WHEN SHE INVITED Peter to stay at the Ancestral Sanctuary Friday evening, he initially protested. But not for long.

"This will be perfect. I did not like to say so, but I have an open return on my plane ticket and I had planned to go back in three days. Because of costs." He stammered. "I mean, I have money, but I do not like to spend all of it on a hotel."

Thelma was equally pleased. The three of them stopped by Peter's motel to retrieve his things. As he walked across the parking lot to tell the owner he was checking out, Digger noted Robert and Elmo near the outdoor Coke machine, staring in Peter's direction, Robert with arms crossed and a deep frown.

Digger couldn't imagine they would care whether Peter was leaving. Unless they had counted on him taking them dining or drinking.

Was it her imagination, or did Peter deliberately avoid looking at them as he slid into the Jeep's back seat?

WHEN DIGGER TURNED off the road into the Ancestral Sanctuary's long driveway, Peter leaned forward from the back seat to stare out the windshield. He silently took in the large flower gardens and two-story house with its circular front driveway.

He kept staring as he took his backpack and a small suitcase from the trunk. "It is stunning. Like American TV shows with rich people."

Thelma smiled. "Digger has added more plants than Benjamin had."

Digger laughed. "I'm very far from rich." She jogged up the steps and unlocked the front door, letting Thelma and Peter precede her into the foyer. Peter glanced up the wide staircase on the left and down the long hall toward the dining room.

Uncle Benjamin slid down the banister. *"Ah. Thelma. And you brought the young man we know little about."*

Digger frowned at him and guided Peter and Thelma to the living room on the right. She enjoyed watching Peter take it all in. The house, the third on the property, had been well cared for since being built in 1878. The refinished hardwood floors looked almost new, and the higher ceiling made the room feel larger than its thirty-two-feet length.

Peter turned to Digger. "You've lived here all your life?"

She shook her head. "I grew up in Maple Grove, but my parents had a house near the elementary school. I inherited this from my Uncle Benjamin a couple of years ago."

Aunt and great-grandnephew settled on the sofa. "He had no children?"

From his perch on the fireplace mantle, Uncle Benjamin said, *"He most certainly did."*

"He has a terrific son, my cousin, Franklin. He works in DC and has a beautiful townhouse in an area called Dupont Circle. He's a city man."

Peter nodded slowly. "In Germany it would be…unusual not to leave the land to a child."

Digger was tempted to say that the money Uncle Benjamin left Franklin more than made up for not getting the large house. "Franklin has an apartment here on the third floor. You'll likely meet him this weekend. We're very close."

Peter's light frown lifted. "I look forward to meeting him." His face brightened. "Your uncle was Benjamin and his son is Franklin?"

Thelma laughed. "People used to tease Benjamin about that, but his late wife, Clara, didn't want Franklin to be self-conscious, so we stopped."

Uncle Benjamin headed for the ceiling. *"I got tired of hearing it, too."* He vanished toward the second floor.

Digger showed Peter to the guest room while Thelma stayed in the living room. While Peter hung up clothes, she took the back stairs to the kitchen to start preparing supper.

Uncle Benjamin appeared in the kitchen as Digger took out a baking dish for the chicken. *"You believe everything this Peter says?"*

Digger spoke in a hushed tone. "I don't know enough to say all of it, but when we were in the library, he showed us the DNA match on Ancestry. I've never heard anyone say that can be manipulated."

"And you checked him out with Sheriff Montgomery. But how much could the sheriff really learn about this Peter from here?"

"I suppose petty crimes wouldn't make it to international records, but we know his passport is accurate. He was born in Cologne, Germany, and lives in Heidelberg now." She pointed finger at him, teasing. "You thought inviting him would be a good idea."

"I still do, mostly."

As she put the chicken in the oven, Digger could hear Thelma's delighted laugh. Delighted, but tired. She was in her eighties, after all. "Come to the living room with me. Unless you want to act as the oven timer."

"No thank you." Uncle Benjamin floated ahead of her and perched on the arm of the stuffed chair Digger sat in, across from Peter and Thelma.

While the chicken baked, Digger listened to Peter explain his family's history and how he descended from Thaddeus Zorn.

"My grandmother, Bridget Schmidt, was born in 1945," he nodded to Thelma, "same as you. This was seven months after my great-grandfather's death in the Battle of the Bulge. Though my family opposed the Nazis, having an American soldier's child was not a popular thing, even at the end of the war."

"You'll never really know what his family thought. A lot of Germans would say they fought on the 'Eastern Front,' which meant they fought the Soviets not the Western Europeans. I bet that was a lie for more than half of them."

Digger didn't doubt him, but she tried to unobtrusively glare at him. She wanted to keep listening to Peter.

"So, Great-Grandmother Marta Durkin kept her romance with Thaddeus Zorn a secret from everyone in town. Of course," he flushed, "everyone could see she was with child."

"Did you know she didn't marry the baby's father?" Digger asked, quietly.

Thelma's eyes widened and she looked at Peter.

"Marta, Bridget's mother, eventually married Jeremiah Schmidt, when Grandmother Bridget was just a few months old. I was later told people assumed the father of her child was a German soldier who died in the fighting."

With mildly shaking hands, he took a drink from the glass of water Digger had given him. He nodded to Thelma. "I didn't know the name Zorn. It's a German-sounding name, but it would not have been a good idea to put an American name on the birth certificate in 1945."

"I can understand that," Digger said.

"Until I was in college, I assumed Jeremiah Schmidt was my mother's grandfather, my great-grandfather. I have been told he was a very good father to my Grandmother Bridget." He smiled. "There are photos of him holding Bridget. He looks happy to be her Papa."

Thelma buried her head in her hands, shoulders shaking. Peter's mouth opened in a wide O, and Digger moved to sit on the other side of Thelma. She put her hand on the woman's shaking shoulder, but didn't initially say anything.

"He shouldn't have said that!"

Digger smiled at Peter. "It's just a lot for Thelma to take in."

"I should not have..I should have," Peter stammered.

Thelma removed her hands from her eyes and sat up straight, a tear still on each cheek. Digger grabbed a tissue from the end table and passed it to her.

"I'm happy, Peter, really." She dabbed at each tear, and it was her turn to reach for a glass of water. She swallowed and smiled lightly. "I am glad to know you, but in the back of my mind I always worried that Thad's child, his daughter, had been unwanted, treated badly."

His look of chagrin lightened. "I showed you pictures of Bridget with her mother Marta, but I did not bring one of her with Jeremiah. I did not think of it." He placed a hand on Thelma's other shoulder. "I believe he loved her very much."

Thelma blew her nose. "I'm glad to know that."

Digger returned to her stuffed chair. "So, your grandmother was Bridget Schmidt. Who did she marry?"

"My Grandmother Bridget married Martin Seneker, and they had my mother, Maria. She married Leonard Becker, and here I am." He smiled, broadly."

Even with a practiced family history ear, Digger had a hard time keeping the names and generations straight. She stood and moved to Uncle Benjamin's old desk, which still sat in the corner of the living room, minus all his files, which she had moved upstairs. She took a notebook and pen from a drawer and returned to sit across from Thelma and Peter.

"So, Peter, I know you have all this on the pedigree charts you brought, but I need to write just the names and generations. Tell me if I'm doing this right."

She jotted names and Peter filled in dates until they had a list both were happy with.

- Thad Zorn, b 1920 and Marta Durkin, later Schmidt b 1922
- [Marta married Jeremiah Schmidt (born 1923) and her daughter Bridget used that name.]
- Bridget [Zorn] Schmidt (b 1945) married Martin Seneker (born 1944)
- Maria Seneker (b 1967) married Leonard Becker in 1988
- Peter Becker, born 1992. Thad's great grandson!

He smiled broadly and leaned over to kiss Thelma on the cheek. "And now I have met my great-grandfather's family and have Aunt Thelma."

Uncle Benjamin pinched his nose with his fingers and moved between them.

She flushed, but smiled. "And I'm glad you found me. I wish you could have met my brother Theodore. He only died in the past year."

Peter frowned. "Do you mind if I ask, did he look like my Great-Grandfather Thaddeus?"

"When I looked at those photos, I didn't think so," Uncle Benjamin said.

Thelma cocked her head and reached for her album, which sat on the coffee table. She flipped it open. "Not a lot like him. I think my brother Thomas looked more like Thaddeus." She shrugged. "I wish I had more pictures of your great-grandfather. And that I had met him, of course."

"It is absurd, but I forget that you did not know him."

Digger glanced at the captain's clock on the fireplace mantle. The chicken needed another fifteen minutes. "You said you didn't find out about your grandmother's biological father until you went to college?"

He nodded. "I went to Heidelberg University, to get a degree in International Studies. That's the town where Jeremiah Schmidt was born. I liked that connection, but it wasn't the reason I went there."

"Good academic program?" Digger asked.

"Heidelberg Schloss. Castle. Mostly called Heidelberg Palace now. My parents took me there when I was young, and I pretended it was a magical place." He flushed.

"That's a bunch of bunk. He made that up."

"I love that," Thelma said.

"Huh. If Thelma likes it, I guess it's okay."

Digger nodded. "And when you were in college, you looked up information on the Schmidt family in Heidelberg."

"Very smart," Peter said. "I made the genealogy quest even then. I found the address of the house where he grew up and walked by it a few times. I hoped I'd see the owners in their garden sometime, and would introduce myself."

"That makes sense," Thelma said.

He nodded. "Anyway, when I was home in Cologne for Christmas, I told my parents this. They looked at each other kind of oddly, and then explained that, technically, Jeremiah Schmidt was not my grandfather."

"I bet he was mad at them for lying to him."

"I hope that wasn't too hard to hear," Thema said.

"Mostly I was mad that they did not tell me before he died." He paused. "I did not tell them that. I do not know that I would have talked to him about it. I mean, he never knew Bridget Schmidt's first father."

Digger smiled to herself. She liked the expression first father. *"I may have to like this guy, even if he did worm his way into our house."*

The doorbell rang, and she stood. "That'll be Marty. He needed to finish something he was working on at the paper." She walked to the foyer, opened the door, and kissed him lightly as he came in.

"I smell something good," Marty shrugged out of his lightweight jacket and hung it on the coat tree in the foyer.

"Baked chicken and I'm about to put on some frozen corn and stick some rolls in the oven." She looked beyond Marty.

He laughed and reached back to the porch. "I brought dessert. Apple pie and vanilla ice cream."

"You are the best." She smiled as she took them from him. "Our guests are in the living room." She led Marty to them. "Thelma, Peter, here's my good friend Marty again."

Peter stood to shake hands, and Thelma smiled from her seat on the couch. "How are your grandparents, Marty?"

"Malcolm and Maria are doing well." He sat in the chair Digger had vacated. "I've been trying to talk them into moving into the senior condos, but they don't want to do that yet."

"Me either!" Thelma said.

Digger had met his grandparents several times. Uncle Benjamin told her he'd called them the Double Ms. She knew Marty's parents lived near Baltimore, where he used to live, but he never spoke of them. The couple times she'd dropped hints that she'd like to know more about his family, he'd veered away from the topic.

Peter asked what senior condos were, but before Marty or Thelma could tell him, Digger headed for the kitchen. "I'll call you guys in ten minutes or so for dinner."

She walked through the dining room, noting she had put out plates but no silverware. She had left her phone in the kitchen and saw its text message indicator flash.

Franklin's note said he would be there by eight instead of later, and asked if Peter had decided to stay at the Ancestral Sanctuary with Digger.

She texted back. "Yep. He turned in his rental car today. Must not be worried about getting stuck in the sticks. I'll keep the food warm for you."

THEY WERE STILL SITTING at the dining room table Friday evening when Franklin arrived. He kissed Digger and handed a bottle of Chardonnay to her and Riesling to Marty before shaking hands with Peter. "I wasn't sure what part of Germany you were from, but I figured a Riesling would be a good option."

"You can always count on my son for classy wine," Uncle Benjamin said. He hovered not far from Franklin, eyes only for his son.

Marty passed the bottle to Peter, whose eyes shone brightly as he regarded it. "Yes, thank you so much."

Digger should have figured her more urbane cousin would think of something like a wine associated with Germany. Franklin had traveled in Europe between undergraduate and law school and had been back a couple of times with friends.

Digger stood and took wine glasses from the top of the buffet behind the table. "Can I make you a plate, Franklin, while we get Marty to pour the wine? We just finished dessert so the chicken's still warm. I'll fix you a plate."

Franklin kissed Thelma on the cheek, and grinned at Digger. "That'd be great. Long week."

He sat across from Peter. "What part of Germany are you from?"

"Cologne, in the Rhine Region. But I went to school in Heidelberg and mostly lived there after university."

"I've visited Heidelberg," Franklin said, as Digger made for the kitchen, with Marty following.

The door swung closed behind them and Marty put a pile of dinner plates in the sink. Then he took a stack of salad bowls from Digger, placed them on the counter, and drew her to him for a long hug. "Next time you have to sit next to me so we can play footsie under the table."

She gently pulled back from the hug. "Then I'd never keep track of what to put on the table."

Marty lowered his voice. "Where's the pale guy?"

Digger giggled. "You know he promises to tell us when he comes in a room. No risk he'll barge in now, with Franklin in the dining room."

Marty began filling the sink with water and dish soap. "Peter's happy he came up here?"

"Yes." Digger told him she recognized one of the men at the motel from her high school in Maple Grove. "He was a jerk then and doesn't seem too different."

"He didn't recognize you?"

She shook her head. "He was three or four years older. You know upperclassmen don't pay attention to freshman. And I no longer have braces or glasses."

Marty turned off the water and frowned. "No reason to think the guy would look for Peter here?"

"Can't see why he would." She took the plate from the microwave. "I'll give Franklin his chicken and be back in a second."

When she walked back into the dining room, she realized how incredibly tired Thelma looked. Of course, she would. It had been an enjoyable, but long, afternoon and evening. Digger put his plate in front of Franklin.

"Thanks, cuz. Have a seat."

Digger smiled at him and turned to Thelma. "I'm stealing Thelma to sit in the living room." To her, she said, "These guys are going to talk German history for a few minutes. Let's grab a more comfortable chair."

"Good idea. She's been looking peaked. I'm staying with Franklin."

Digger nodded in acknowledgement, though anyone would have assumed she was doing so toward Thelma.

Peter appeared chagrined. "I've been ignoring you." He stood and pulled Thelma's chair back from the table.

"Not at all," Thelma said. "I enjoy listening to all of you. But I could do with a little rest."

When she stood, Digger extended her crooked elbow. "Allow me, madam." She grinned at Franklin. "If Marty comes out here to see why I'm not helping with the dishes, point him to the living room."

Digger led Thelma to the stuffed chair across from the couch. "Better head support. You look as if you might want a nap."

She sat, gracefully, and leaned into the chair. "To be honest, it's almost my bedtime."

Digger sat across from her. "I should have thought of that. Why don't you let me drive you down the mountain? You can leave your car here and Marty and I can bring it to you tomorrow."

Thelma shook her finger toward Digger. "I'm not an invalid, young lady." But she smiled, clearly tired.

Marty came in. "I heard that. Digger and I could drive you down. It'd be like a date," he gestured his head behind him, "while those two get acquainted."

Digger nodded. "One of us can pick you up tomorrow for a late breakfast. It'll be Saturday, and we can figure out what more you want…"

A strong knock on the door startled all of them. "Goodness," Thelma said.

Digger began to stand, but Marty pointed to the couch. "Probably somebody who has a flat tire and saw the lights." He opened the door and, surprise in his voice, said, "Good evening, Sheriff Montgomery."

"Evening. Sorry to just stop by."

Digger stood. She doubted that. Roger Montgomery was a very purposeful man. She gestured that Thelma should stay seated and headed for the foyer. "Come in, Sheriff. We have apple pie and ice cream."

Marty shut the door behind Montgomery as he came into the foyer.

He patted his girth. "Nope, I've sworn off. I'm on a mission for my grandmother."

"I call her Maryann the Troublemaker," Marty said.

He shook his head. "She is that."

"Come in and sit down, Sheriff," Digger said.

He knew where the living room was, so entered and greeted Thelma. Digger shrugged at Marty as Franklin and Peter came out of the dining room.

Peter wore a frown. Perhaps police didn't stop by homes in Germany.

"Peter, Sheriff Montgomery is also a friend."

The two men shook hands. Montgomery smiled. "You look like your passport photo."

"Everything okay?" Franklin asked.

Uncle Benjamin swept past them and into the living room. *"If the sheriff is here, it must be trouble."*

Without thinking, Digger said, "Not necessarily."

"Really?" Franklin said.

Digger could see Marty holding back a laugh. She added, "I meant it doesn't necessarily mean something's wrong. Let's see."

Franklin gave her a questioning look and turned his attention back to the sheriff.

"Gotcha," Uncle Benjamin grinned.

Digger indicated the sheriff should sit on the sofa, and she and Marty sat there, too. Franklin and Peter pulled two straight-back chairs from near the fireplace to be close to the others.

Sheriff Montgomery nodded to Peter. "We spoke on the phone, of course."

Peter, seeming nervous, smiled. "Yes. Thank you for starting my introductions."

Montgomery nodded. "That was a good way to go about it." He looked at Thelma. "I check in on Grandmother Maryann every couple of days, and I mentioned that it looked like Peter was Thelma's grandson, or great something." He looked to Peter. "My grandmother lives up here now, but she's originally from where Thelma's family lived, in Oakland."

Thelma sat up straighter. "Of course. She was my sister Therese's age. I haven't had a chance to visit much with Maryann since she moved from Oakland up to Maple Grove."

Montgomery glanced at Digger and Marty. "As you know, my ninety-year-old grandmother is still as sharp as somebody your ages." He pulled an envelope from his pocket and handed it to Thelma. "She thought you'd like to have this."

"Goodness," Thelma said. She removed a photo and her eyes filled with tears as she studied it. Then she held it out to Peter. "This may be the best picture of your great-grandfather that you'll ever see."

CHAPTER SIX

SHERIFF MONTGOMERY ENDED up driving Thelma home after an emotionally charged trip down memory lane for Thelma and, ultimately, Peter.

Digger had scanned the photo, which showed Maryann with Thelma's sister, Therese, in Halloween costumes. They looked about age ten, and behind them was a smiling Thaddeus Zorn, who looked to be eighteen. He dangled car keys above their heads as he looked into the camera.

Digger printed a paper copy of the now-scanned photo for Peter. She promised him they could print a better version on her office printer.

Peter could hardly stop looking at the photo. He finally spoke. "Thelma said she had so few pictures of Thaddeus – she calls him Thad, doesn't she? – because people didn't take many back then."

"It's true," Marty said. "But maybe Maryann's father took it because the girls were dressed up for Halloween. It's lucky Thelma's older brother was in the shot."

Franklin took the picture from Peter to study it. "So, Thelma wasn't born until later?"

"Would you call Thelma an afterthought or a mistake?" Uncle Benjamin asked.

"In 1945." Digger said. "It says 1938 on the back of the picture, so Maryann and Therese were eight, and Thad would have been about eighteen."

Franklin smiled and handed it back to Peter. "Looks as if he was their ride to a Halloween party."

Peter kept staring at it.

"What I don't get," Marty said, "is why Sheriff Montgomery drove out here on a Friday night? How did he know we'd all be here?"

Franklin smiled. "I asked him that when I walked him and Thelma to his car. I don't really know his grandmother, but she must have the kind of antennae my dad had."

Uncle Benjamin had been behind Peter, studying the photo, but his head whipped up to regard his son.

Franklin continued. "The sheriff said Maryann was in the library late today, and the librarians were excited about Peter and Thelma finding each other. She asked questions, of course."

Digger finished. "And the librarians knew I invited Peter up here for the next few days."

"I get that," Franklin said. "But it still doesn't explain why he drove up here."

"You can tell he doesn't know Maryann well."

Marty looked at Franklin but pointed at Digger. "You know how you and I have said we wished your cousin was a little less curious?"

"They also say nosy, but that's only if you aren't in the room."

Franklin grinned. "I seem to recall talking about that."

"Hey," Digger began.

"Now," Marty said, "multiply her inquisitive nature times two, and you have Maryann. Once she put a bug in the sheriff's ear and that photo in his hand, he had to come up here."

"She's also," Digger began.

Peter interrupted. "Do you three know how lucky you are?"

Digger's brow furrowed, but she figured it was a rhetorical question and waited for him to continue.

"Say what?" Marty asked.

"You have, you have family." He glanced at Marty. "Okay, he's not already family. But you are close. And you know all these people well enough that they…they drive up a mountain in the dark to see you."

Digger realized she didn't know if Peter had siblings or other family he was close to. "We are lucky."

"Me, especially," Franklin said. "My parents were older when I was born…"

"He was a surprise, not a mistake," Uncle Benjamin said.

"...and I have no brothers or sisters. I'm twelve years older than Digger, so mostly she was a pest when I was in high school. Now we're good buddies." He smiled at Digger and she made a heart with her fingers.

Peter frowned. "So, Digger, your parents were also old when you were born?"

"Actually, Franklin's father was my father's uncle. He was my Grand-Uncle Benjamin."

Uncle Benjamin looked wistful. *"Technically, I still am."*

"Since he was my father's uncle, Franklin and I are first cousins once removed."

"And Digger does have a sister,' Marty said, "but she and her husband and their two children don't live near here."

"We're in regular touch,' Digger added, "though this Thanksgiving will be the first time they're coming up here since COVID happened."

Peter nodded. "I am an only child. I have two cousins from my father's sister, but we are not close. I used to wonder why we didn't see them much. I tried to visit one of my cousins, a girl named Helga, in Frankfurt a few years ago. She was polite, but always busy." He paused. "My mother finally told me that people in the family were angry at my great-grandmother for being," he flushed, "pregnant with the child of an American soldier."

"That's stupid," Marty said. "And it was a long time ago."

Peter sat up straighter. "You are of course right, but my father's family's home was destroyed in the war, in Berlin." He spoke quickly. "Not that they thought Hitler was right. But they lost everything, including my father's aunt."

"That would be hard," Franklin said. "There are people in this country, mostly in what we call the border states, who are still angry about incidents from our Civil War. And that was in the 1860s."

Peter started to say something, but Franklin yawned and stood. "I was up at five-thirty AM so I could get to my law office at seven-thirty. Peter, if you're interested, I'll drive you to Civil War sites tomorrow. There are a couple places not far from here that played a part in that awful war."

"That would be wonderful. Would Thelma want to come?" He asked.

"Not too likely," Digger said. "I'll bet she asks us to come to her place tomorrow, though."

Peter looked at Franklin. "Gettysburg? Everyone has heard of it."

Marty raised a finger. "I'll bet you didn't know the railroad bridge at Oakland was blown up in 1863. By Confederate soldiers, not Union."

Franklin yawned again. "Excuse me. We can look at a couple of things in Oakland. I was thinking of Harpers Ferry, West Virginia, but we'll have to see how much time you have. 'Night all."

As he got to the bottom of the steps leading to the second floor, Franklin looked at Digger and drew a question mark in the air.

She knew he was asking if his father was going to come upstairs with him. She moved to the landing, smiled, gave a short nod, and spoke quietly. "You can talk to him, which he would like. If it creeps you out, after a while, tell him you'd like him to head to his old room. I do it all the time. He doesn't mind."

Franklin stared at her. "That's why you haven't moved in there?"

"A little bit." She smiled.

To others in the living room, it would have seemed that Ragdoll jumped off the table in front of the window to follow Franklin upstairs. In reality, the cat was following Uncle Benjamin, who slid up the banister in front of Franklin.

DIGGER WAS IN THE kitchen about to start the coffee pot on Saturday morning when Uncle Benjamin called from the dining room. *"I want credit for remembering to tell you I'm coming."*

She smiled, and spoke softly. "Sounds good."

He floated in through the swinging door to the dining room. *"I want you to tell Franklin about some Civil War history materials he should take with him today. For Peter to look at. I can tell you where they are."*

She flipped the brew switch. "It's pretty complex history, especially for someone who didn't learn U.S. history in school. Franklin will explain things well."

"That's why it's good to have something to read." He said this as if Digger was missing a basic point.

"You know the floor-to-ceiling bookcase I had built along the living room wall, next to the half-bath? I have a couple things there, but the best might be a short booklet that describes the Confederate raid into Oakland in April of 1863."

"When they blew up the railroad bridge."

"Right. What if we just give him that one? Franklin said he'd take Peter to Oakland."

The back stairway that was in the hallway behind the kitchen creaked and Franklin appeared, looking around. "I can guess who you were talking to. Is Peter still upstairs?"

"Yep. Thanks for offering to take Peter around today." She concentrated on the brewing coffee. There was no reason to feel so awkward when Uncle Benjamin was in the room with the two of them. But she did.

Franklin stared at her before opening the fridge and removing a carton of orange juice. "You're going to be feeding a bunch of people this weekend. You should let the lawyer contribute."

Digger smiled at him. "I let the lawyer pay all of the cost of building an apartment for himself in the attic."

He gestured toward her with the OJ. "That's different. And now that you're looking at me, are you okay?"

She pushed the brew button on the coffee maker. "I wish there were a way for Uncle Benjamin to talk to both of us. It feels… stiff sometimes."

Franklin's eyebrows went up. "Was it easier before I knew?"

"Maybe, just a little, sometimes." She grinned. "But the guilt was killing me."

"Don't let it get you. We don't need two ghosts around here."

Uncle Benjamin looked panicked. *"We might not be able to leave the house!"*

FRANKLIN PACKED A LUNCH for himself and Peter and they left the Ancestral Sanctuary at nine-thirty, with Peter driving Thelma's car, which she had left there the night before. They would drop it at her house and do their Oakland sightseeing in Franklin's car.

As they pulled out of the driveway, Digger called Maryann Montgomery. "I don't know if your grandson told you what a hit that photo was last night."

"I haven't talked to him, but Thelma called this morning. She thanked me so much I told her if she did it again, I wouldn't look for any more photos of her sister, Therese."

Digger laughed. "If you have more, she'd love them. Peter, her new great grandnephew, is going to stay here for a few days. Maybe you can come up here or meet us at Thelma's."

"I'd love that. She invited me to dinner. My late brother's grandson, Brian, is here today, but he's going back to college this evening."

Digger said goodbye, turned on her laptop, and opened it to the folder that had the copies of the letters Thelma had received from her brother Theodore. She glanced around the room. No Uncle Benjamin. He'd probably want to look at the letters, but she didn't want to wait for him to show up.

Marty stood behind her as she pointed to the screen. "I didn't have time to go over them, but I did divide the scanned copies by letters Thomas wrote to Therese and those she wrote to Thomas. She must have thought the letters would mean something to her descendants, because a bunch of those are carbon copies of what she wrote to him. If he kept the originals, they didn't make it to Thelma."

"Nothing from those two to Thelma?" Marty asked.

"Not so far. I plan to ask her. We also have a few letters Theodore wrote to Therese. I guess all the letters ended up with him after Thomas and Therese died. Thank goodness she was a pack rat and he kept them, too."

Marty grinned. "Pot calling the kettle black. I've seen your history files."

Uncle Benjamin appeared near Marty's elbow. *"Mine were even better. Bigger stacks of them, too."*

Digger ignored him and spoke to Marty. "True. How do you want to go through these? Should I give you copies on a flash drive?"

Marty took his laptop from a bag that sat on the floor near the mahogany buffet. "Yeah, and then maybe we could each read a few of Thomas' and Terese's letters and compare what we think."

"Good idea." Digger popped a flash drive into her laptop, copied the scanned letters, and handed it to Marty. "Help yourself to coffee anytime."

Uncle Benjamin hovered at Digger's shoulder, but said nothing.

Digger began with the oldest letter, one from Therese to Thomas in 1992, when she was age sixty-two. She began by telling him that since she had broken her foot and couldn't visit the next month as planned, she wanted to write about some of the things she remembered and see if he remembered them the same way.

Digger skimmed the chit-chat and Therese's report on her health.

From Therese to Thomas, May 1992

I remember how hard Dad worked at that hardware store. Every night when he got home, he'd sit in that high-backed chair in front of the fireplace and Mother would rub his neck for two or three minutes. Then she'd bring him a beer. Remember, he only wanted National Bohemian Beer?

In fourth grade, I had a lot of trouble with long division. I think I would have had less trouble if the teacher had let me write the number to carry over at the top of the next column. Anyway, Thad helped me, and after he went to the war Dad did. No matter how tired he was.

Mother didn't like it when he had to do that. She would say if they still had their farm and dairy cows he wouldn't have had to work in "that drafty store," that I shouldn't ask for help.

Dad usually didn't say anything when she talked about the store, except one time you and I were both doing homework at the kitchen table and they were in the living room. She said something about the store and it was bad for his back, and he told her she should remember they were lucky he had that job, and besides, milking cows was hard on his back, too.

Then they started arguing, and I ran upstairs so I didn't hear it. Mom blamed Dad about something with selling their house, and that's what started the yelling. Do you remember what they said?

From Thomas to Therese, June 1992

He began by asking her about her foot and then telling her about his rheumatism, which he said was only really bad when it was damp and cold. Then he answered her question.

What I remember most is that Dad did not like to talk about them having to sell their house and land for the lake. Mother didn't either, of course, especially since her parents built it. Dad didn't mind as much because her parents had left them the farm and he always felt beholden to them. He told me that much later.

Her father was still alive when they got the money, and Dad tried to give him some of it. Grandfather Giacommo wouldn't let him. He said he'd throw the money in the creek. Dad believed him, so he stopped trying to force the issue.

Before he left for the War Thad told me a lot of things. It never occurred to me he wouldn't come back, but I guess he knew a lot of guys died over there.

Thad wasn't sure whether to believe everything Dad told him. He thought maybe his mind was getting foggy or something. Anyway, Dad said the house wasn't supposed to be submerged, just close to the flooded parts. He was angry about it. Thad eventually went to the county courthouse and looked at the maps from that Eastern Land Corporation. They had a line that almost went through the property. Thad thought that meant flooding was likely, though he could see how Dad might have misread it.

Anyway, that's kind of what Mother and Dad talked about that night. They also talked about some things that got left behind, but that's for another letter.

When she finished Thomas' letter Digger looked up and met Marty's eyes. "What kind of surprises me is how perfect their sentences are. On the 1940 census, I saw Thad worked as a clerk at the newspaper. Maybe they all worked with words."

"What surprises me," Uncle Benjamin said, *"is that he left his sister hanging, the way he ended that last letter."*

Marty spoke before Digger could respond. "I think Thelma was a teacher. You told me the 1950 census is online now. You can look them up later if you really want to know." He nodded at his laptop. "I want to see what was left behind."

Therese to Thomas, June 1992

In the next letter to Thomas, his sister largely castigated him for not giving her many specifics about things that might have been left behind.

And besides, as mom would have said, I think it's poppycock.

Love,

Therese

"I think Thomas' initial response to her is in that first letter I scanned. The one that's so faded it didn't have a readable date. It talked about Thad seemingly telling Thomas about their mother's sapphire ring." Digger went to Thomas' next letter, which she judged to be his third.

From Thomas to Therese, July 1992

I know you always want a lot of detail. I've been trying to think more about it.

Of course, this Left Behind stuff isn't mysterious, and it's what Thad told me that Dad told him. So, who knows?

The house in town was smaller than that big farmhouse. Mother had a bunch of brothers and sisters, plus they had a room for farmhands at the back of the house, for when it was real cold.

Mother and Dad moved their furniture and what Dad called 'everyday things' to the house in Oakland, but a couple things they were waiting to figure out how to fit them. Mother had some big ol' loom her mother had used to make thread from sheep wool. I hear it was kind of a hobby for her more than because they couldn't buy thread.

There used to be a picture of it, but I don't know where it went. Course, the loom was wood and old. It would have been destroyed by the water right away.

Thad said that Dad was worried that with them moving into the house in town – which he had built, you know – that they would attract attention and that could attract burglars. So, he hid some stuff at the old place. Me, I'd have worried people would go into a house they thought was vacant, but it was pretty far out of town.

Anyway, you know how stories get spread and maybe embellished. Thad said Dad had some tin boxes made – there used to be a traveling tinsmith who came to town until maybe 1940. Dad had a bunch of gold coins. When they sold the farm, he wouldn't take what he called paper money, so he was paid in coins.

"That's taking caution to an extreme," Uncle Benjamin said.

Digger thought about that. Surely, he put some in the bank. Not in an account, but in a box. Would an Oakland bank have had safe deposit boxes in the 1920s? Probably. If not, the concept originated with private companies, and he could have leased a box in one of those.

Marty's voice brought her out of her thoughts. "Did you get to the part about the coins?

She nodded. "Either a bank or one of the private security box firms could have held gold coins for him. I think the bank was the Garrett National Bank of Oakland."

"Maybe because he was out in the country, he didn't want to drive into town with it."

"Maybe, but they were moving into town." She went back to the letter.

Thad said Dad put some of those coins, mom's sapphire ring I told you about, and some gemstones in tin boxes. He buried them in the foundation, on the outside, near the largest chimney. Supposedly with a flagstone over them. But he didn't dig them up before the place flooded because he didn't expect the house to be under water. And they'd only just moved to town, because it took longer for the people building the new place to finish it.

I didn't really believe Thad at first. But after he was killed, I wondered if he told me so someone would know Dad's secret.

So now you know. What do you think?

Your brother,

Thomas

Digger again looked at Marty. "Weren't you going to see exactly where the Zorn's farm was?"

"Yep. I found the area on an old map that's on the wall in the courthouse. But it was hard to relate it to where the waterline is today."

She grinned. "I have a map that shows before and after on the same map." She stood. "Be right back." She went up the front staircase, entered her room, and reached under her bed.

The map she'd bought had superimposed today's roads over a lighter map that showed the old election districts and lines that indicated what the lake now covered. She had pinned it onto a large piece of commercial ceiling tile that she had covered in modern burlap-type fabric.

She pulled it out, went downstairs, and placed it on the large dining room table. "Does this help?"

"Huh. I've never seen this."

"A real estate firm here made it, or commissioned it. I found it on the Internet."

Marty studied it. "I suppose if you were from here, it'd be easier to decipher what part of the map is for today and what's the old boundaries."

Digger traced a brown line. "I think this is where land was in the early 1920s. Now the lake is there."

Marty wiggled his eyebrows at her and his glasses slid down his nose. "Land's still there. Just wet now."

"Man after my own heart," Uncle Benjamin said.

"Funny. We still don't know exactly where the Zorn family farm was, but I think really near Thayerville."

They huddled over the map, which had today's lake, highways, and towns as the top layer. Under it were light-colored boundaries and election district markings.

"I see what you mean," Marty said. "I'm not from here, and I get this, but can't figure out all the before markings."

"You need to get a highway map from back there. I have old Rand McNally maps."

"Old maps? Where?" Digger asked.

Marty didn't ask who she was talking to.

"Come to think of it, they're in my son's room, in boxes under that…oh, wait. If you didn't toss everything in the closet in my old room, there's some in the very back, on the top shelf."

To Marty, she said, "Maps might be in boxes at the back of Uncle Benjamin's old walk-in closet, but I don't remember seeing them."

"Let's check," Marty said. "Lead the way, Benjamin."

Digger laughed and her eyes followed her uncle's back as he whizzed toward the stairs behind the kitchen. "He's already on his way."

They walked hand-in-hand up the main staircase. "You have no idea what a relief it is that you believe Uncle Benjamin is real."

He hesitated. "It was hard. I mean, he pushed those papers off the table so I'd see them. But I also hear you ask him history questions, or you repeat comments he makes about people much older than us. It all…reinforces it."

Uncle Benjamin stuck his head out of the wall in the upstairs hallway. *"Hurry up, slowpokes."*

Digger jumped and he pulled his head back.

"He doesn't usually talk to me from the walls. I think he found something in the closet."

CHAPTER SEVEN

They walked into the master bedroom, which Digger had repainted light beige with a dark burgundy chair rail. Uncle Benjamin hated it, but she had reminded him he no longer slept there, and she needed it to look different.

However, she had kept the antique oak furniture, which Aunt Clara picked out. She had replaced his modern-looking black headboard with a wood one with oak veneer, but made sure it had shelves for his books about Maryland history. The tall, oak chest of drawers still stood across from the bed, but the bedside table no longer had piles of papers and books.

Light streamed in from the huge picture window that overlooked the vegetable and flower gardens, but they walked into the dark closet. Digger flipped the light switch and walked to where Uncle Benjamin sat on a tall shelf in the back.

"I thought I looked up there."

"You probably did, but these aren't big map books, they're folding maps." He turned his head. *"Far back on the shelf and pretty old paper."*

Digger looked to Marty. "The maps are on the second shelf up, probably beyond even your reach. There's a stepstool in the linen closet in the hall."

He made an exaggerated sigh as he left to get the stool. "I have to do all the work."

Uncle Benjamin whispered, *"He's a keeper."*

Digger laughed. "You don't have to whisper. He can't hear you."

"What am I missing?" Marty asked.

"He likes you."

"Tell him I don't want to put a ring on *his* finger someday."

Uncle Benjamin cackled.

Digger flushed. "Ooh boy."

Marty patted the top of her head. "You're still safe. Now, point me to these maps."

They were so fragile, Digger didn't even take them from him, but let him carry them to the dining room table and spread them. "We should take pictures of these because this may be the last time they can be opened without disintegrating."

They studied the old map and then the current one.

"Gee," Marty said, "Part of Meadow Mountain basically went beyond Thayerville. Now the lake is there."

"So's the mountain. Just more of the lower altitude is under water." Uncle Benjamin said.

Digger ignored him and traced with her finger. "And there's Deep Creek itself." She looked at a photo Marty had taken of the plats of land in that area before the lake was filled. "Maybe the Zorn family property was about here?"

"Look it up on the 1920 census," Uncle Benjamin said.

"On the census before the lake," Digger said. "I should have thought of that."

"How will that help?" Marty asked.

"It won't be a perfect comparison, but usually census tracts don't change much, especially in small towns. I'll look at the 1920 and 1930 censuses and see what tracts are different in 1930. You know, no people."

She opened her laptop and went to census.gov, then opened her own family tree. She had already included pages from the 1920 and 1930 census records with her family, so she didn't expect to have to look hard to find a starting place in Garrett County.

But it was harder than she thought. She found census records and they noted the tract, but – unlike for 2020 – she could not find a map of the 1920 tracts for the entire county.

Frustrated, she went to the Garrett County Historical Society to browse maps. In the Virtual Map Room was exactly what she needed – a 1924 map of roads to be relocated for flooding of Deep Creek Lake. Bingo.

"Look at this map, Marty."

"Me, too," Uncle Benjamin said.

He peered over her shoulder. "I'll be darned. I didn't even know about that virtual map site."

"I'd forgotten about it," Digger said. "We don't need to know the precise boundaries of the Zorn farm. The future lake was going to cover all of the main roads east of the town of Thayerville."

Marty whistled. "I get that it's not like submerging Annapolis or Baltimore. But looking at that segment of the county shows dozens of miles of road that would soon be home to fish, not people."

"Literally, hydroelectric power is progress," Digger said. She closed the virtual map page. It's certainly no secret, but I think it would take too long to orient Peter to the old roads versus current ones, and he doesn't really need to know the differences."

"Agreed."

Uncle Benjamin said nothing, but frowned at the computer.

"What's up?" Digger asked him.

"If I could go into the Garrett County Historical Society site on my own, I'd never be bored."

"I know. Wish you could." Digger told Marty what he had said.

Marty was about to respond, but the front door opened and Franklin called for Digger.

"We're in the dining room," she said.

"Making a mess," Marty added.

Franklin and Peter joined them. "I wouldn't expect anything else," Franklin said.

He glanced at the maps and turned to Peter. "Without even asking, I can tell they're trying to figure out where the Zorn family used to live."

Peter had appeared exhausted, but he perked up. "Where, exactly? Can you show me?"

Marty stood aside so Franklin and Digger could look more closely. Franklin frowned. "I'm not sure it matters so much where it was. It's under water now." But he studied the highway map, Marty's photo of the plats, and the new map of the lake.

"But not in the middle of the lake?" Peter asked.

"No, not at all." Franklin put his finger on the newer map. "If you get out one of those tourist maps, it'll show you a couple of hotels on the lake in Thayerville. But what's left of the old town itself is just a crossroads. A couple small stores. I think the convenience store is more of a liquor store."

Peter nodded. "It is just so odd to think of their land under water."

"From what Thelma thinks, it's not all of their former property. Maybe one of the hotels, or at least its marina, sits on former Zorn cow pastures."

Marty studied the newer map again. "This isn't far from where those two yahoos were practicing their scuba diving a few days ago."

Digger smiled. "But they wouldn't have been looking for so-called sunken treasure."

Peter sat up straighter. "Treasure?"

"Which Thelma doesn't seem to believe was there," Marty said. "We saw some letters between some of her older siblings, and they alluded to maybe some small boxes buried near the farmhouse foundation. She didn't seem to put a lot of stock in their stories."

"What happened to the men who were on the lake after dark?" Digger asked. "Did the magistrate release them without bond?"

"It was a misdemeanor, so he did," Marty said. "But when I tried to find them early Friday morning, they had checked out of their hotel."

Uncle Benjamin snorted. *"They better have left good forwarding information with the courts. You can get in a lot more trouble for ignoring a summons to appear than for being on the lake after dark."*

FRANKLIN, USED TO WALKING across town to his office and working out, came home from serving as a Saturday afternoon tour guide in good form. Peter seemed exhausted and took a nap.

Marty went home, and would meet them at Thelma's later.

Digger and Franklin leaned against the kitchen counter drinking iced tea. Uncle Benjamin sat on the red-topped table and beamed at both of them.

"What do you think of Peter?" Digger asked.

"Seems a nice enough guy. For the first half-hour, all he could talk about was his – what is he, great-grandfather? – and how amazing it was that he found Thelma. Eventually he figured out I wasn't the family history buff you are, and…"

Uncle Benjamin interjected, and Franklin stopped, aware Digger seemed distracted.

"Do you think now that Franklin knows I'm here that someday he'll be able to see me?"

Digger glanced from Uncle Benjamin to her cousin. "He wants to know if I think someday you might be able to see and hear him."

"Dad, this is a lot newer to me than to you two. It would be great, but it's been close to two years since you died. Or whatever you call it."

Digger grinned. "I used to call it resurrected, but he kind of developed a savior complex. I told him to knock it off."

"I'm serious, you two."

"I know you're serious, Uncle Benjamin. I think we have to…stay alert to the possibility. If Franklin starts to, I don' know, see flashes of color whiz by, he can ask me what you're wearing that day."

Peter spoke from a few feet away. "Flashes of color?"

Digger gawked at him.

Franklin recovered faster. "We were talking about how colorful Garrett County history was. Still is colorful."

"I guess it's all a lot more interesting to us than someone from Germany," Digger said

Peter glanced from Digger to Franklin and back to her. "I read that booklet you gave me about the Civil War raid in Oakland. I did not know how crucial the B&O Railroad was in supplying the soldiers who supported your President Lincoln."

"We talked about how fast the railroad bridges were rebuilt after the Confederate troops destroyed them," Franklin said.

"I do not know a lot about trains built in Germany, but they would not have had to go so many miles."

"Wish I could have been there to explain how we used to have a lot of small railroad lines all over the place," Uncle Benjamin said.

Franklin nodded to Digger. "We were near the old Depot in Oakland, so we went into the transportation museum and looked at some of the older photos of bridges, especially drawings of the railroad bridge. That didn't take long, so I drove Peter up Highway 219 so he could see some of the vacation places close to the lake."

Digger thought their conversation sounded stilted. "Sounds fun."

He shrugged. "I visited Heidelberg that summer between undergrad and law school. Peter could talk about that city for hours."

"Franklin asked me to meet him over there. But I said I was too busy with the store." Uncle Benjamin shook his head. *"The things I thought were important."*

Digger poured her remaining ice cubes down the sink. "I'm going to make a thing of coleslaw to take to Thelma's, so it isn't all store-bought food.'

"May I help?" Peter asked. "And what is cole slaw?"

"It's a cold salad, made with mayonnaise and cabbage. You can watch," Digger said.

Franklin glanced at his watch. "I'll head down before you do so I can get that rotisserie chicken I ordered from the grocery store." He grinned at Peter and tilted his head toward Digger. "I know. And rolls, and broccoli you can cook after we get there."

"You are trainable. Marty said he'd bring dessert and pick up Maryann Stevens, the sheriff's grandmother. It's great she knew Thelma's sister."

DIGGER WAS FAIRLY certain Thelma's house was a Sears Craftsman bungalow. She thought of them as early modular homes – delivered on the B&O Railroad and taken by wagon or truck to the site on which they would reside for decades, if not centuries. She had heard some homeowners had the skills to assemble them with relatively little help.

Twilight highlighted the large, deep red front porch surrounded by white railings, still with hanging baskets of flowers. Most were tired geraniums or petunias, but the chrysanthemums in front of the porch bore brilliant burnt orange, red, and yellow blooms.

As they got out of the car, Peter sniffed the air. "I wish I could bring the scent of your mountain air to Germany. It is different than ours. Maybe because your lake is not far away."

Uncle Benjamin walked to the mums and tried to pick one, frowning when he could not. *"I think that's overkill. We already know he likes the place."*

Digger smiled as Marty parked his Toyota behind her Jeep Compass. "I'd offer you a jar to store it, but I'm not sure it would travel well."

Peter laughed, and as Marty got out of his car, he told him what Digger had said.

Maryann smoothed her skirt. "And what would you tell the people at German Customs about the jar?"

Digger grinned as Marty locked his car door and ambled toward them, camera strap over his shoulder. "You keeping those two in line, Maryann?"

"I hear her stories," Peter said. "Digger should perhaps watch out for her. Or watch her."

"Agreed," Marty said. "So, Peter, I wondered if you'd mind if I did a story about your visit. There'd be a lot of interest in you and Thelma finding one another, and what you learned about each other's lives."

Peter seemed to almost stumble.

"I don't think he likes that idea," Uncle Benjamin said.

"Probably you should ask Aunt Thelma. She stays after I go."

"Marty doesn't do hatchet jobs," Maryann said.

Peter looked at Digger.

"He doesn't sensationalize a story." They had reached the porch steps. "And it would be okay to tell him to leave out your grandmother's name, or something like that."

Marty jogged up the steps and opened the screen door. "Absolutely. We don't want your family back home to think the *Maple Grove News* is like London's *Daily Mail*."

DINNER AT THELMA'S was the sort of polite meal among people who don't all know each other well. Friendly and well-mannered. Franklin and Peter had both gotten lost near the Eifel Tower in Paris, with Franklin eventually finding himself near Notre Dame.

From his spot sitting cross-legged on Thelma's buffet, Uncle Benjamin said, *"I remember this story."*

"They aren't so close together," Peter reminded him.

"True," Franklin said, but they're both tall and I could see Notre Dame from my hotel. I didn't realize I was looking from the other direction, so after I walked from the Eifel Tower to the cathedral, I still had a long walk to my hotel."

After dinner, Franklin and Marty moved the coffee table into the dining room so there would be more room for long legs. They seated themselves in Thelma's small sitting room, Peter between Digger and Franklin on the gray camelback sofa and Marty on the floor near Digger. Maryann and Thelma sat in Queen Anne chairs across from the sofa.

Maryann took in the entire space, and Digger bet she thought the muted colors – in fact lack of any bright colors – reflected sadness on Thelma's part. She supposed if she were the last of her siblings and had no children that she might be sad, too.

As they sat, Peter's phone dinged as it had at least twice during dinner. He smiled sheepishly at Digger after he typed a very short reply. "My mother is awake either very late or very early."

Digger nodded. "Parents like to know what's going on."

From his perch behind Franklin, Uncle Benjamin said. *"So do uncles."*

When they were settled, Maryann spoke first. "Thelma, I look forward to swapping stories with you for a good while, but now I'd love to know if you think there's treasure buried in the lake, by your parents' old place."

Marty leaned toward Digger and spoke softly. "Never need to wonder about an elephant in the room when Maryann's around."

"I may need a cane, but my hearing's not so bad," she said.

"You got me," he said, and flushed.

Thelma spread her hands across her lap. "I only heard my parents allude to anything buried once, and I didn't understand what they were talking about. Some letters that just came to me seem to say that my brother Thomas and sister Therese had heard those stories. It just seems so unlikely that my father would leave anything behind."

"Even more unlikely," Franklin said, "that he'd not try to find someone to look for the items, assuming they had some value beyond being keepsakes."

"Did you tell Maryann where the house was?" Marty asked.

"My parents' property was near Thayerville, which is not much of a town anymore. A good part of it is under the lake."

Peter frowned. "They buried houses, trees, farms? All of it?"

"Make sure you tell them how many trees were cut down."

When Thelma didn't seem ready to answer, Digger did. "A utility was to build the dam, which created the lake by damning up the Youghiogheny River by Deep Creek. That company hired a firm to buy the land from people who were going to lose their property. Or at least lose access to it."

"*Eastern Land Corporation,*" Uncle Benjamin said.

"So," Digger continued, "people sold. Some were able to move their houses to another part of the county, but Thelma's parents didn't think the house would do well if moved."

Thelma nodded. "That's what my father was told. That's when the family moved to Oakland. It was 1924 or 1925."

"And even a lot of vegetation was cut down," Franklin said. "Thousands of trees were removed."

"I wonder what they did with all that wood," Uncle Benjamin mused.

"Why did they care about the trees?" Peter asked.

"I know this," Thelma said. "They talked about it in my biology class in high school. There actually are underwater forests. An area is dammed up, like here, and the water is cold enough to preserve them. But they didn't want that for our lake. At the time, I don't think they knew how much recreation there would be, but it would have been bad for boats and fishing."

"Plus," Maryann added, "Those were tall trees. In some places, they would have been above the water line."

Peter nodded slowly. "So, everyone was happy?"

Thelma shrugged. "People were more accepting of things like that one-hundred-years ago. Plus, electricity was spotty in the mountains then. Everyone liked getting electricity."

"That's all true," Maryann said. "I'm fifteen years older than Thelma. Some still complained when I was a little girl. Not so much as time went by."

Peter's eyes widened. "You are more than ninety?"

"She doesn't look a day over eighty-five," Uncle Benjamin said.

Maryann tossed her head. "A lady doesn't tell her age."

As Peter flushed, Marty and Franklin laughed. "She's pulling your leg," Marty said.

"Ah. I've heard leg-pulling is another way to say joking."

"Your English is so good, I forget you aren't a native speaker," Digger said.

"I acted in plays in school. When I studied English pronunciation, I told myself it was like learning a French accent for a play. You have to do it perfectly."

"Very smart," Maryann said.

Peter cleared his throat and reached for the ever-present backpack, now on the floor at his feet. "I never saw Deep Creek Lake or knew the story of it until my visit, but I…well, I have not shown this to Aunt Thelma yet." He looked at her and she smiled.

Digger saw Uncle Benjamin dive into Peter's backpack. He didn't usually explore personal property, but she wouldn't mind knowing what else was in there.

Thelma looked exhausted. Digger realized they probably shouldn't stay much longer.

Peter took a see-through plastic bag from the backpack. In it was a worn-looking air mail envelope with red, white, and blue lines around the edges.

Digger recognized it as one made of paper almost as thin as onion skin paper, and it looked old. Then it hit her. These were like envelopes World War II soldiers sent home; they had copies of many such letters in the Maple Grove Historical Society. Only one person's letters from that time period would be relevant to Peter and Thelma.

With care worthy of a copy of the Declaration of Independence, Peter handed the letter to Thelma. "This was in my great-grandmother's things. But I only saw it a few months ago, after my grandmother died."

Digger couldn't be sure, but it sounded as if Peter's grandmother might have died about the same time as Thelma's brother, Theodore.

Thelma slid the letter from the plastic bag and studied it. Then she drew in a breath. "This is addressed to Marta Durkin. Is that APO address from my brother?" She traced the address with a forefinger.

Digger sat very still. As Thelma grew paler, she began to stand to go to her, but Franklin was faster. Gently he took the letter from her hand, which had begun to tremble. "Why don't you lean back, Thelma? This is a lovely surprise, but it might still be something of a shock."

"Yes." She rested her head on the upholstery. 'I, uh, thank you, Peter. I, you've read it of course." She had begun to regain her composure.

Peter's eyes had widened and his posture stiffened. "I'm sorry, I thought…"

Thelma spoke more firmly. "It's a wonderful surprise." She looked up at Franklin. "Why don't you read it for us?"

Franklin always had an air of assurance. Digger figured it was probably why Thelma chose him. That and the fact that he now held the letter. Franklin glanced at Peter, who nodded and leaned into the couch.

Franklin stayed on his feet. "It's dated December 12, 1944. Gee, that would be just before the Battle of the Bulge."

"He died in that battle," Thelma said, softly.

Franklin's eyes widened. "I didn't know. I'm sorry." He went back to the letter.

My love Marta,

I write this the night before we leave. You know I wasn't allowed to tell you when, and I don't know when we'll be back. But you and I will be together in spirit, always. And soon in person, I hope.

You asked if I told my parents about you. They will like you, I know, but I will have to wait until the war is over. Your parents hate the Nazis, but not as much as my parents. Well, maybe they do more than mine. But I can't tell my parents I'm in love with a German girl right now. You know I will stay in Europe until I can bring you home with me.

For now, look in our favorite spot in the holzschuppen. You'll find something there to keep you company until we see each other again.

I love you forever.

Thaddeus

Digger's eyes were moist and her nose ran. Thelma had already pulled a tissue from her pocket. She managed to say, "Such a treasure."

Peter's expression showed obvious relief. "I have a copy at home, and one with me." He nodded to Thelma. "This one is for you. It should stay in America."

Marty asked, "What's a holzschuppen?"

Thelma spoke before Peter did. "It's a woodshed. My grandfather spoke English, of course, but he used that German word for the lean-to on the farm, where he stored firewood."

"My goodness," Maryann said. "We may have just learned where Peter's grandmother was conceived."

Uncle Benjamin came out of the backpack with a loud cackle. *"Even I wouldn't say that."*

CHAPTER EIGHT

MARTY SPEWED AN ICE cube several inches in front of him and quickly retrieved it to return to his glass of ice water.

Franklin's eyes met Digger's, and she knew he wanted to laugh, but held it together.

Maryann appeared chagrined. "I meant no disrespect."

Thelma grinned broadly. "None taken. I wish I'd met her."

Digger could feel Peter relax. "She would like to have met Thaddeus' little sister."

Thelma looked at Franklin and held her hand out for the letter, which he returned. "I'm sure my parents would have loved your Grandmother Bridget. And Great-grandmother Marta, of course." She paused for a moment. "Being German-Americans, my parents always felt they needed to apologize for Adolph Hitler. But they certainly didn't hate all Germans."

Thelma smiled as she fought a yawn. "I do want to spend more time with you." She put her hand over her mouth and yawned. "My goodness, my mother would have made me skip dessert if I'd ever done that at the table."

That led to a flurry of "we should go" and "it's getting late" comments.

Peter hesitated as he stood and looked at Thelma. "I'm not sure how long I'll stay, but I hope I can see you again."

The yawn had vanished. "My goodness, yes."

After several seconds of silence, Marty asked, "What are your immediate plans, Peter?"

Peter zippered his backpack. "I do not think I will stay much longer. My mother sends me texts every day."

"Are you an only child?" Maryann asked.

He nodded. "I get all of her attention."

"She misses you," Thelma said.

Peter smiled. "She is used to me being in another town, but not across an ocean." He frowned lightly. "And she reads always about people being killed in America. With guns. She does not understand how peaceful it is in the mountains of Maryland."

Marty rose from his spot on the floor. When he didn't think anyone was looking, he shook a finger at Maryann and she shrugged.

As they traipsed out the front door, Uncle Benjamin said, *"There's a lot of interesting stuff in that backpack."*

PETER WANTED TO RIDE back to the Ancestral Sanctuary with Franklin to ask more questions about the Civil War near Oakland. Marty had his car and would drop Maryann at her apartment, so Digger and Uncle Benjamin were alone in her Jeep. "What did you mean about interesting stuff in Peter's backpack?"

Uncle Benjamin sat on the dashboard to face Digger. *"He has what you'd expect for a tourist: a sightseeing map of Maryland from the Visitor's Bureau in Annapolis, a couple souvenirs he bought in Oakland."*

"Not too interesting," Digger said.

"Two cell phones, which probably makes sense when you're in a foreign country and the one from home might not work here. But he also has a map of Deep Creek Lake and a pamphlet on boating safety."

"He didn't mention he wanted to go onto the lake. Maybe I should take him to a marina that takes tourists for rides."

Uncle Benjamin moved to the passenger seat. *"You could offer, of course. What struck me funny is it was a navigation map of the lake. Why does he care how deep it is in one place versus another?"*

Digger slowed as she turned onto Crooked Leg Road and kept her eyes on the unlit, winding road. Why did Peter have a navigation map? He couldn't have been one of the two men trying to scuba dive. Marty must have seen their pictures at the sheriff's office. Besides, Peter wouldn't have heard any stories about gold coins buried at the foundation of the old Zorn farmhouse.

"No comment about the maps?" Uncle Benjamin asked.

"People buy those because there's more detail about the lake itself than fun things to do all around it. You know, like where the dam is, not just the road over it."

"If you say so." Uncle Benjamin floated through the front window and sat on the hood. *"I'll watch for deer for you."*

PETER WENT UPSTAIRS to bed as soon as they got home. Digger, Marty, and Franklin walked into the kitchen, Digger intending to make a cup of tea for them. Uncle Benjamin was already sitting on the table when they entered.

Franklin turned to Marty. "Would you mind if I borrowed my cousin for one of our walks down the driveway?"

Marty yawned broadly. "I think I'll head upstairs."

As he made his way up the back stairs, Franklin looked at Digger. "Okay if we go alone?"

"Sure." She turned to Uncle Benjamin.

He floated off the table. *"Sure. We should develop some sign language for later, so you can give nonverbal cues when you want me to vamoose."* He headed up the back stairs after Marty.

Digger grinned and told Franklin what his dad had said. "I could give him the raspberries."

"Did I hurt his feelings?"

"No. Not only is he used to me asking him to buzz off sometimes, he really does respect others' need for privacy."

They went down the back steps, Bitsy ahead of them, and began their long trek down the gravel drive. After a few moments, Franklin said, "You probably wonder why I've been a little off at times."

"Not too much, but you also said you'd had a long week."

"I'm working on a complicated patent case. But part of it involves who benefits from the invention after the patent-holder's death. Lots of fingers in the proverbial pie."

Digger waited. She couldn't see where he was going with this. She picked up a stick from the driveway and hurled it to the right. Bitsy took off after it.

Franklin took a deep breath. "Okay. I'm going to sound mercenary. But it's kind of the opposite. I really am glad that Dad left you the Ancestral Sanctuary. I've already spent $50,000 of that big chunk of change he left me building an apartment into the dingy basement of my townhouse on Dupont Circle and updating the kitchen and bathrooms."

She smiled. "So, next time I visit, the shower in the one on the third floor will work?"

"More likely than not." Bitsy returned with the stick and Franklin automatically took it from him and threw it to the left. "I also love coming up here. Even more than when Dad was alive. I loved the guy, but what we had to talk about was…the past. I mean, I asked about what was going on around town, and he was happy to tell me."

Softly, she said, "I don't think he cared what you talked about."

"Probably not. But now, it's you and Marty, and I like your friend Holly, and we go out to eat sometimes. It's just, I don't know, more like the real world."

"I think I get it," Digger said. "We can hang out, but you also have your own space up here."

"That's true." He smiled. "Don't kick Marty to the curb."

Digger slapped him on the elbow. "I like him." When he smiled, she asked, "Do you remember any of the people I dated in high school or college?"

He looked surprised. "I'm sorry, I don't. I guess we didn't see each other as much."

Digger shook her head. "Because I didn't date. I had friends and we did a lot, but I didn't have a real date until after college."

"Oh, I'm sorry."

"But I'm not. I had lots to do. I was just quiet. If I really 'needed' a date, like for someone's wedding, I'd ask one of the guys I was buddies with, like Cameron or this guy Jerry. I liked my life."

They took a few steps in silence as they reached the front of the driveway and turned back to the house.

"I guess I understand that making a commitment is a big deal," Franklin said. "Should be for everyone of course."

"And I would do it for forever," Digger said simply. "Everything has to be right."

Bitsy returned with a different stick. Digger threw it and the shepherd took off.

"As long as you don't expect perfection," Franklin said. "You have to have give and take."

Digger nodded. "Of course. Umm, I don't think this is why you've seemed a bit unfocused."

Franklin smiled. "Yeah. You're in charge of your love life. I want to ask, and it's a stupid question, sounds selfish…"

"You aren't selfish," Digger said.

"What will happen to the Ancestral Sanctuary if you die before I do?"

Digger stopped walking abruptly, so Franklin did, too. She started again. "Gee, my will just says, I mean right now it says, anything I own goes to my sister. Then I have a list of personal things to go to specific people. I didn't even have a will until after Uncle Benjamin died, and I saw how much easier it was to settle his estate because he had one."

"Would your sister and her family move here or sell it?" Franklin asked.

"Oh, I think I know where you're going. I could, uh, ask her to reimburse you for the cost of building the apartment…"

Franklin waved a hand. "I don't care about that at all. It's just…all of a sudden this place means more to me than it ever did. I love coming up here."

"Okay," Digger stopped walking again. "I guess there's the issue of Uncle Benjamin, too."

"Gosh. I never thought about that."

Digger grinned. "It's hard to forget him when he gabs at you a lot."

Franklin said nothing.

"Okay. Like they say in communication classes, I hear you. I need to think. I, wait, what do you want to happen if I die first?"

"I'd like the right of first refusal to buy it. With the money going to your sister, of course. Or her husband and kids if she's passed. And I figure we'll all live for decades."

With his use of the legal term 'right of first refusal' the conversation suddenly felt very mercenary to Digger. She tried to push that thought aside.

"You know, it's a bigger issue if I do get married and have kids."

"By then, our lives will be so different I may not care. And, it will rightfully belong to your husband and kids."

"Or you could be married with kids." She touched his elbow with hers. "You'll probably want the master bedroom then. Even if I'm still kicking."

"I don't…I shouldn't have brought all this up."

"It's good to talk about it." Digger tried to keep a rising chill from her voice. This didn't feel like one of their driveway talks, which always brought her comfort. "We just have to sort some things out."

BITSY NEVER LET Digger sleep past six AM. On Sunday morning, a cold nose woke her, rancid breath panting with excitement. She pushed Bitsy's head away from her and regarded his alert shepherd's ears. "Okay, okay."

She slid out of bed into slippers and Bitsy bounded for the bedroom door.

"Better you than me," Marty mumbled.

Digger stretched, glanced at Ragdoll's empty bed in the corner, and padded after Bitsy. Uncle Benjamin wouldn't enter her bedroom unless invited, but if Ragdoll's bed was empty, she could be sure he was elsewhere.

They went down the back stairs and Digger watched from the porch as Bitsy did his business near the largest flower bed. He wouldn't try to head for the woods before chowing down. After he'd finally sniffed near several of the graves in the small family plot, he galloped toward the house.

"Okay, Boy, you've earned your breakfast."

Bitsy came up the porch steps and into the back hallway. Tail wagging, he loped into the kitchen.

Digger thought Franklin or Marty must have gotten up, and was surprised to see Peter puzzling over the coffee pot. "Good morning. You're up early."

He smiled absently and returned to studying the coffee pot. "I am very sleepy until I drink coffee, and my maker is very different than this one."

"Let me feed Bitsy and I'll make it."

He moved to the kitchen table and sat. "I'm sorry to be more trouble."

Digger poured dry dog food into Bitsy's bowl. "No trouble. I'm making some for me, too."

Peter studied his phone as Digger started the coffee pot and put four mugs on the counter. "I'm heading upstairs to get dressed. Help yourself to creamer and juice."

With his gaze on his phone, Peter smiled and said, "Thank you very much."

Digger freshened up and dressed in jeans and a tee shirt that said, "Tree hugger in chief," with an image of a huge tree with a couple headstones under it. She could hear Franklin in his bathroom on the third floor.

She rapped on her bedroom door as she went by. "Rise and shine." She moved quickly down the front staircase and opened the blinds in the living room windows.

In the kitchen, she greeted Peter again as she opened the refrigerator door. "Scrambled eggs okay?"

Peter looked up from his phone and spoke in a hurried tone. "I have an open-ended return ticket to Germany. I may need...I mean, I wouldn't want to...I may need to begin my travels today."

Digger turned from the fridge, orange juice in her hand. "That would be a real shame. What makes you need to leave today?"

He was again looking at his phone. "I told you my mother gets worried about me being in America. The newspapers in her town always talk about American gunslingers, or gang wars."

Digger shut the fridge and took down glasses. "What if you sent her some photos of Maple Grove, or Thelma's house? Or the lake?"

He sighed, heavily. "I wish that would help. I sent her one of me and Thelma, at her house. And," he smiled, "of your cat. She loves cats."

Digger nodded slowly, her back to him. "You need to do what you think is best."

MARTY DIDN'T WANT TO join them for the ride to Cumberland, where Peter would take the train to Washington, DC. He did visit Thelma with them, and made an excuse to stay for a few minutes after Digger and Peter left.

As they pulled away from the curb, Peter asked, "Why did he want to remain? I did not have the impression they knew each other so well."

Digger kept her eyes on the road as she turned toward Interstate 68. "We were concerned she would be especially sad. Marty is going to offer to take her to lunch with Maryann."

"Ah. The one who thinks my great-grandmother was conceived in the holzschuppen."

"The one and only."

They were silent for several minutes as Digger negotiated the mountain roads and finally pulled onto the interstate, heading east. She glanced at Peter's profile several times. Either he was worried about dealing with his mother or something else really bugged him.

"Are you happy with what you learned here?"

He turned from the window. "Very happy to have met Aunt Thelma. And all of you, of course. Some people think Americans are only concerned with themselves, but I will be telling my family and friends of your hospitality."

"That's great. If you come back, you'll have a place to stay as long as I have the Ancestral Sanctuary."

"And it is yours because your Uncle Benjamin died and Franklin did not want it, yes?"

"In a roundabout way. The first house was built on the property in the 1850s, I think. This is the third one, the largest, built in 1878. Uncle Benjamin bought it from the estate of one of his ancestors not too long before Franklin was born."

"So, he was not there before?" Peter asked.

"He'd been there many times. I understand there was a big Thanksgiving dinner for all the family for many years. But he didn't own it."

"And," Peter persisted, "Franklin did not want to have it?"

"Uncle Benjamin wanted it to stay in the family, and Franklin had his career and house in Washington, DC. He comes to Maple Grove more now that I live in the house. And," she hesitated, not sure Franklin would want her to talk about his finances, "Uncle Benjamin left him a fair bit of money. So, it...evens out."

Peter nodded. "I see. So, you are both happy?"

It seemed an odd question from someone she didn't know well. "Yes."

Peter stared out the passenger window for another minute. "I told you another day that I am jealous that you have close family."

"Right." Digger adopted a lighter tone. "We aren't many, but we are close."

AFTER SHE DROPPED PETER at the train station, Digger stopped at a bookstore and bought a copy of the Sunday *Washington Post* for Franklin. Maple Grove was too far from DC to have it delivered, and it would be a treat for him to read it before Monday morning. After she bought Marty's grandfather black jellybeans at a candy store in Frostburg, she headed home.

Marty called when Digger was close to Maple Grove. "I have to admit, I thought lunch would be a bore, but Maryann and Thelma traded stories like a couple of drunks on barstools."

"I doubt Maryann would mind the comparison, but I'm not sure about Thelma."

He laughed. "Did you know that when the war ended in 1945, well the war in Europe, that Maryann and one of her friends burned their parents' gas ration books? They thought the end of the war meant the end of rationing."

"Good heavens. But not the food coupons?"

"She didn't mention it. So, how was Peter? I'm surprised he left so soon."

Digger nodded to herself as she drove into town. "Me, too. There must be more to it. Maybe his mother's sick or something, and he didn't want to say."

"I suppose. I'm going to try to make copies of some land records tomorrow for Thelma, then I don't plan to think about the Zorn family history."

"Ditto." Digger said. "I have a feeling Uncle Benjamin will want me to take him to the historical society so he can dive into some books, just because it's Thelma's family."

"What's for dinner?" Marty asked.

Digger matched his teasing tone. "Whatever you're cooking."

CHAPTER NINE

DIGGER AWOKE IN THE DARK. Why was she awake so early on a Monday?

An alarm wouldn't stop ringing. The sound must come from the old-fashioned wind-up alarm clock Uncle Benjamin always used. But she hadn't rewound it.

Her fingers groped the bedside table and landed on her mobile phone, which was buzzing, though not with the old-fashioned ringtone. She sat up groggily and grabbed the phone.

"What is this?"

"Digger, wake up. It's Sheriff Montgomery. I'm on your front porch."

"What are you doing there? It's nighttime."

His voice rose. "Digger. Splash some cold water on your face and open the front door."

"Okay, okay." She swung her feet to the floor and slid them into slippers. As she did, she dropped her phone. "Damn."

She grabbed her robe from the foot of the bed and stood still for several seconds. Franklin was upstairs in his attic bedroom. Marty must have gone home at some point. Why was Sheriff Montgomery here?

Her body started moving again and she was at the top of the staircase before she thought she really should splash water on her face. And she had wine breath from last night's dinner. Hurriedly she doused her face, brushed her teeth, and ran a comb through her hair.

Bitsy sat in the bathroom doorway. "Why didn't you bark?"

She moved quickly down the steps and unbolted the front door. "Sheriff?"

"Lemme in, Digger." He brushed past her. "Your dog is worthless."

"What do you…?"

He interrupted her. "When's the last time you saw Peter Becker?"

"I dropped him at the train station in Cumberland yesterday. What's happened?"

He gestured toward the living room. "I'm not sure."

He moved into the living room without waiting for an invitation and sat on the overstuffed chair across from the couch. Digger sat across from him.

Digger shook her head to get rid of cobwebs. "He was supposed to take the train from Cumberland to DC and fly out of Dulles Airport to go home. Back to Germany." She could feel her heart pounding fast. "Why are you asking about him?"

Sheriff Montgomery pulled a plastic bag from the pocket of his leather law enforcement jacket. "This is a German passport. Very wet, but we were able to slide a paring knife between some pages. It belongs to Mr. Becker."

"Where, where was it?"

"In a backpack that was hanging off a boat in the middle of the lake. An empty boat. Almost looked as if someone tried to throw it overboard and the strap got stuck on the cleat."

Digger could picture the horn-shaped hardware used to secure a rope to a boat, with the other end of the rope tied to the dock. She stared at Sheriff Montgomery. "What color was the backpack?"

"At first we thought it was black, but it was really a deep purple."

Digger stared at the front window. She envisioned Peter's backpack strapped over the back of a chair in the library. She refocused on Montgomery. "That sounds like his. What does it mean?"

"Did he have it with him when you dropped him off?"

"Definitely. He slung it over his shoulder and pulled a suitcase behind him."

Bitsy head-butted Digger's knee and she absently scratched his head. "What does it mean?"

"Could mean a couple of…"

Franklin's voice came from the top of the second-floor staircase. "Digger? Is that you and Marty?"

"It's the sheriff. Come on down."

Franklin, clad in sweatpants and a Maryland Terrapins tee-shirt, came quickly down the stairs and into the living room.

Montgomery stood and shook his hand. "No firm info, just asking questions."

Franklin sat next to Digger on the couch "Information about what?"

"My office had a call from the Department of Natural Resources Police. Right now, we're mostly helping with identification." He repeated what he had told Digger. "And it could mean a couple of things. Maybe someone swiped Becker's backpack when he was sitting in the train station."

"He would have called one of us," Franklin said.

Digger nodded, her mind in turmoil. She had dropped Peter at the station. He wished he could have stayed longer, but he seemed fine. Preoccupied with his mother's concerns, perhaps, but fine.

"The more unexpected option, so to speak, is that Peter didn't get on that train. Perhaps had no intention of doing so, and came back here. Why would he do that?"

Digger turned to Franklin. "I have no clue. Do you?"

Uncle Benjamin stood in front of Digger. *"I might have an idea."*

She couldn't ask him to explain himself, so Digger raised her eyebrows at him.

Franklin turned toward her and then Montgomery again. "He hung on every word Thelma said about her father hiding things near the house's foundation. But he wouldn't," he looked to the sheriff. "Where was this empty boat?"

"He had a diary in that backpack." He adopted a pious expression. *"I didn't read much of it, because diaries are private."*

"Quite a ways from here," Montgomery said. "The boat was about a hundred yards out from a commercial dock in Thayerville."

"What kind of boat? Digger asked.

Sheriff Montgomery stared. "Does he know people with a particular kind of boat?"

"I wouldn't think he had time to meet boaters, but I guess I only know what he told me."

"A jon boat. Twelve feet."

Digger pictured the flat-bottom fishing boat sitting on the lake near Thayerville, a town so small some tour guides called it a hamlet. There weren't many homes on the water, but there was a resort hotel.

"A rental?" Franklin asked.

"Didn't have any markings that said so, and it wasn't in great shape. DNR Police have it."

"Damn," Franklin said. "What the heck was he doing on the lake? Or his backpack, anyway."

"You know the lake better than I do" Digger said to her cousin. "Is that close to where Thelma's parents had their house?"

"From what I gathered from Thelma, reasonably close," Franklin said.

Montgomery said, "I doubt the craft had drifted much. Why would it matter if it was near where Thelma's family lived? They sold that land more than 100 years ago."

Digger shrugged. "Peter and Thelma talked a lot about his great-grandfather. Thelma wasn't born until after he died, but her brother, Peter's great-grandfather, lived in the older Zorn home."

"On a night like this, anyone would have heard even a single oar in the water. Ask him why they looked for the boat."

Digger nodded slightly. "It's a new moon, so it's dark. You said someone heard something?"

Montgomery drummed his fingers on the arm of the chair. "As I said, we got the call from DNR Police. They'd had a call about a loud splash and some raised voices. When they found the backpack on an empty boat, they called down to us to see if anyone was missing. Deputy Jim Collins met the DNR guys, and called me when they realized who the backpack belonged to."

Digger had wondered why the sheriff himself had knocked on her door. If Deputy Collins was at the lake, maybe only one other deputy would be on duty at night.

"Voices, plural?" Franklin asked.

Sheriff Montgomery nodded. "Far as I can gather. DNR has jurisdiction over the lake and its parks, but we work together well. It's early on us looking at this." He nodded at Digger. "You have a way to contact this Peter Becker?"

"I should have thought of that. He has a smart phone, but he bought a cheap flip phone to be sure he always had service in the U.S." She stood. "My phone's upstairs. I'll call him on both phones."

"Do me a favor and call him down here, so I can listen in," Montgomery said.

Digger jogged up the steps and grabbed the phone from her bedside table. She walked down more slowly, scrolling to find Peter's phone numbers.

Franklin called from the living room. "I'm going to wake Marty to see if he's heard from Peter." He stepped into the foyer with his phone.

Digger sat on the couch and put her phone on the coffee table, tapped Peter's number, and pressed the speaker button. It rang three-and-a-half times and the voicemail picked up. He spoke in German, presumably asking her to leave a message. She glanced at the sheriff.

"Leave a neutral message."

The phone beeped and she said, "Peter, this is Digger. Just checking to see how the train ride went. You're probably in the air now. I should have called earlier." She pressed the end call button. "That doesn't really tell us anything, does it?"

Montgomery shrugged. "Only that he's not answering that phone, wherever he is. Try the flip phone he got here."

Digger repeated the process, with the same result. "The flip phone had sixty minutes or something, but I think those phones let you retrieve messages even if you're out of minutes."

Franklin reentered the living room from where he'd gone to make his call. "Marty hasn't heard from him. He wondered if we needed him up here."

"Ask him what else was in the backpack," Uncle Benjamin insisted.

The sheriff snorted. "All I need is a reporter tailing me."

Digger cleared her throat. "Peter had some notebooks, and I gave him some granola bars to put in the backpack. Did you find anything besides the passport?"

Sheriff Montgomery's phone buzzed and he held up one finger. "What's up Collins?" He paused, listening. "Uh huh. Okay. Sure. I'll meet you at the hospital in Oakland." He stood.

"Is Peter okay?" Digger asked.

"*He didn't answer your question about other items in the backpack,*" Uncle Benjamin said.

"They found a body face down in the lake. It's the middle of the night, so DNR Police asked our ME for help, and they're bringing it to our hospital. I don't know who it is."

CHAPTER TEN

DIGGER AND FRANKLIN SAT at the kitchen table, saying little. Uncle Benjamin sat on the other side of the table, Ragdoll by his side.

"When did you start letting the cat sit on the table?" Franklin asked.

"After I threw her off the hundredth time. She only sits in that one spot."

Franklin reached over to scratch the top of her head. "She always did have a mind of her own."

From where he sat next to her, Uncle Benjamin said, *"Same as her owner."*

Digger started to say something, but her phone buzzed with a text from Marty. "Leaving the hospital. Coming your way." She glanced at her watch. Four-thirty AM.

"Marty's on the way up from the hospital. Don't you think he would have said if the body was Peter's?"

Franklin hesitated. "Probably. Listen, Digger, I'm sorry I brought up that stuff about what would happen to the house. I feel like there's a wedge between us."

She had felt some awkwardness, too, but certainly not a big divide. "I don't feel that way. It's just so much to think about. And then there's the legal stuff. Whatever we do has to be done right." She smiled. "I know a lawyer."

Franklin smiled tightly. "The lawyer you know would like to pay for any and all legal services, but you should get your advice from a neutral attorney."

A car turned into the long driveway and flashed its headlights.

Digger stood. "Marty. Maybe he knows if it was Peter." She walked to the Toyota's driver's door as Marty alighted. "Was it Peter?"

"I didn't see the body, but I had a couple photos of Peter on my phone, from that dinner at Thelma's. Sheriff examined them himself to remember exactly how Peter looked. After he swore me to what he called 'short-term-secrecy,' he said the person was darker, almost olive-skin color, and more solid than Peter." He gave Digger a quick hug.

They walked arm-in-arm to where Franklin stood.

Franklin shook Marty's hand. "So, we know Peter wasn't the body in the lake, but we still don't know where he is or why his backpack was on the boat. Is the sheriff looking for Peter?"

"He's got the lead on finding Peter, since he seems not to be in the lake or parkland that DNR manages. Sheriff's going to have someone call the airlines. If Peter wasn't on a plane, he'll ask the state police to watch for him. Right now, Montgomery and the DNR Police are more focused on figuring out who the body is."

They climbed the steps, Digger feeling as if she could use another five hours or so of sleep. "I wonder if it could be one of the two guys who stayed at the Oakland Motel, near Peter's room." She glanced at Marty. "Remember I told you one of them was a few years older than I am?"

"Who?" Franklin asked.

"Robert Thorn," she said. "He'd be a lot younger than you. And Peter was uncomfortable around him. That's one of the reasons I invited him up here."

"Maybe it's one of the two who were caught playing scuba diving a few days ago," Marty said.

"Maybe both of those guys at the library were the divers," Uncle Benjamin said.

"One of the scuba divers, anyway," Franklin said.

Digger nodded at Uncle Benjamin so he'd know she heard him.

"Didn't you see photos of the guys caught on the lake a couple days ago?" she asked Marty.

"Nope. Just the names." He took out his phone and began to text as he walked."

Bitsy, who had been sleeping by the living room hearth, jiggled the tags on his dog collar as he stood. As Digger slowed to pet him, she realized Ragdoll was not with them, and she didn't see Uncle Benjamin anymore.

The three of them sat at the kitchen table and Marty's phone beeped.

"Did you hear back from the sheriff?" Digger asked.

Marty read something on his phone and grunted. "Apparently, I'm no longer covered by having sworn secrecy. He said they're following up on the man's identity."

Franklin stood. "Listen, Digger, if I leave now, I can still beat the traffic around Hagerstown." He glanced at Marty. "Early birds heading to DC."

She nodded. "Sure."

As he went upstairs, Marty gave Digger a puzzled look. "You guys okay?"

"We're fine. We just had an odd conversation about…future history." She forced a smile.

Marty didn't ask for details, and five minutes later, Franklin walked quickly down the front staircase. "Cuz, you down here still?"

Under her breath, Digger said, "He knows I am." More loudly, "Yep." She pushed through the swinging door to the dining room and Marty followed.

In the front hallway, she gave Franklin a quick hug. "Thanks for being here when they found that body."

"Glad I was. Let me know when you learn about Peter." He pulled from her and held out a hand to Marty. "I'm glad you're here." He turned and hurried to his car.

They stood at the front door and watched Franklin head down the driveway. Digger looked up at Marty. "It doesn't matter about traffic in Hagerstown. Today is the Columbus and Indigenous People holiday. He just wanted out of here."

Marty regarded her. "Maybe you can talk more about whatever it is next time he's up here."

"Maybe." Digger wished she told Franklin she liked his idea. If she looked into it a lot more and didn't like it, she could tell him then.

To herself, she muttered, "It wouldn't be something hanging over our heads."

Marty poured a cup of coffee. "And that's the kind of seemingly ad-hoc comment that will make anyone else think you've lost it."

Digger fought tears of frustration. "It's not something I can talk about just yet. I mean, no one's sick or anything."

Marty took a swig of coffee and returned his cup to the counter. "I'll get my laptop from the car, and you help me figure out if we can learn more about Peter's life in Germany."

"That's not what's bugging me."

"I know, but it's a task we can do something about."

FOR THE NEXT HALF-HOUR, Digger watched Marty search for information on the Internet as she talked to Uncle Benjamin about the diary he'd seen in Peter's backpack. *"I don't believe it belonged to Peter. Or, he didn't write it, I mean."*

"If the passport got wet, any diary in there would have been soaked, wouldn't it?" Digger asked.

Marty glanced up. "Montgomery said the backpack hung halfway in the water and half in the boat."

"He had it wrapped in paper, inside a plastic bag," Uncle Benjamin said. *"If it didn't stay sunk for a while it might be readable."*

Digger repeated that to Marty. She added, "Uncle Benjamin said he didn't read much of it because it was private."

Marty kept typing. "Heck of a time for him to stop being nosy."

Digger smiled and turned to Uncle Benjamin. "Tell me more about the diary. Why don't you think it was Peter's?"

Marty stopped typing. "If it wasn't Peter's, whose was it?"

Digger put her hand to her mouth. "Oh my God."

"What?" Uncle Benjamin asked.

"In Thad Zorn's last letter to Peter's great-grandmother..."

"Damn." Marty said. "He left something for her, Marta, wasn't that her name? In the woodpile, when he left."

"Huh," Uncle Benjamin said. *"I believe it was his. It wasn't too mushy. I looked at the last page, and he said he would be back for her and drew something that looked like a mountain."*

Marty had shut his laptop. "I'd rather hear about this."

"Not much to say. If we can get to it again, I'll go through it." Uncle Benjamin paused. *"Now that I think of it, it was less a diary and more a description of home. Here. Maybe he wanted her to know what their lives would be like in America."*

"In case he didn't come back," Digger said.

"If you take me to the sheriff's office, I could probably find it in a file cabinet or something and read all of it."

Digger turned to Marty, who looked frustrated not to be able to hear the conversation. "It may have been written by Thaddeus more to tell Marta about here rather than record Thad Zorn's life. The only way Uncle Benjamin can read more of it is if we stop by the sheriff's office. Uncle Benjamin could sneak into their evidence room, or whatever they call it."

Marty opened his laptop. "I'm going to look for more background stuff on Peter. The Europeans don't give as much access to criminal records as we do."

"Did you expect to find something?" Digger asked.

"What he's doing now is pretty shady," Uncle Benjamin said.

"You don't know that he's doing something shady," Digger retorted.

"Actually, if Peter's not on a plane or at the bottom of the lake, he's up to something," Marty said.

Digger sat back in her chair. "Why don't you sign into my Ancestry account? I also have a subscription to newspaper databases. I pay for some European papers because I'm doing some research on my mom's family now."

"If you're giving this guy access to your Ancestry account, you should probably marry him," Uncle Benjamin said.

Digger flushed. She met Marty's amused expression.

"He's being a jerk," she said.

"Made you blush." Uncle Benjamin cackled as he floated upward. *"I'm going to find my cat."*

Digger sat, thinking. The most positive explanation would be that Peter's backpack had been stolen before he got on the train in Cumberland. But he would have called not just to tell her but because he didn't have his passport. Scratch that idea.

Why such an elaborate ruse if he didn't want to continue to stay at the Ancestral Sanctuary? And why go onto the lake at night? The best explanation for that was that he had believed the story of buried items at the now-flooded Zorn farmhouse and come to look for himself. But that seemed so far-fetched.

How would he have known about it? The little diary? Why not simply show it to Thelma? And how had he found people with a boat willing to go onto the lake at night?

Marty interrupted her thoughts. "I may have found an article about Peter in Heidelberg. Can you open your laptop so you can look up some words in a German dictionary?"

"I, uh, could. But I don't think you have to make it that complicated. Copy the text and email it to me." She retrieved her laptop from the living room.

Wordlessly, Marty emailed the text and she opened it. Digger then copied it and went to Google Translator. "What paper is this from?"

"It's from Heidelberg," Marty said.

Digger told Google to translate the two paragraphs from German to English. She didn't expect what she read. "Come over here and look at this."

Marty stood behind her. "Wow. Who in their right mind would even try to shoplift a diamond bracelet worth 30,000 Euros?"

Digger glanced at the date. She guessed that would be a few years after Peter got out of college. If he even went to college. "The picture's blurry, but it looks like him. It says he went into the jewelers with a story about buying it for his parents' fiftieth wedding anniversary."

"No gift for his father?" Marty asked, sarcastically. He bent closer to Digger's laptop. "Someone else came in and demanded the shopkeeper's attention. With that distraction, Peter supposedly slipped the bracelet into a pocket and told the store owner he'd come back in a few minutes."

Digger could smell Marty's aftershave. "That's pretty lax security."

Marty noted the name of the jewelry story and put it into a search on his laptop. "Again, it's in German, but there's a photo of the owner in front of a very tiny store. Looks like an old building. Someone's giving the old guy a bouquet of flowers. Must be some anniversary."

Digger shut her laptop. "It mentions he was from Cologne, which is where Peter's parents still live, I think. It doesn't matter if we find more. This tells us more about who he is."

CHAPTER ELEVEN

DIGGER'S EYES FLEW open only two hours later Monday morning. Her first thought was, "Thelma." She felt guilty about not calling her, but what would she say? Peter might be at the bottom of the lake? And by the way, he might have come here to steal from your family. That could give even a young, healthy relative a heart attack.

Marty stirred. "If you're getting up, holler at me in half-an-hour."

She slid her legs over the side of the bed. "Will do. I don't promise hot water."

He smiled slightly but didn't open his eyes.

Digger grabbed clothes, paying little attention to her choices, showered, dressed, and headed to the kitchen. The heavy feeling in her stomach worsened as she saw a tiny magnifying glass next to the sugar bowl on the microwave. Franklin had given it to her after she had found out who killed a man who lived in a cabin on the mountain.

Her phone beeped from where it sat on the kitchen table. She had forgotten to take it with her when she went back to bed.

A text from Sheriff Montgomery asked, "Have you heard from Peter Becker?"

Digger checked her email and phone messages and texted back. "No. What do I tell Thelma?"

"I'll handle it. Will ask Grandmother Maryann to sit with her, if Thelma wants."

Aloud, Digger said, "Good idea." She reached into the cupboard for coffee and plugged in the pot.

A morose Uncle Benjamin floated into the kitchen and sat next to the coffee pot. *"Will you talk to Sheriff Montgomery today?"*

"He just texted to see if I'd heard from Peter. I don't know if he'll organize any kind of search today. If he does, I'm going down to the lake."

"Are you going to your office? Founder's Day is a federal holiday you know."

"I don't get paid leave."

Uncle Benjamin seated himself on the table and Ragdoll joined him. *"I didn't finish telling you about what I saw in Peter's backpack. I wouldn't mind going through it again."*

"More? What was it?"

Bitsy trotted into the kitchen and woofed for breakfast. Digger took a large bag of his food from the pantry and put some in a bowl.

"The thing is, it was private. I see a lot of things I don't talk about."

She wrestled the dog food bowl to the floor to keep Bitsy from overturning it. "Like what?"

"If you would update your check register more regularly you wouldn't have to worry about an overdraft."

"How…? That was one time almost two years ago."

He shifted uneasily on the table. *"Peter showed you all the letter his great-grandfather wrote to his great-grandmother, before he went off to fight in the Battle of the Bulge."*

"Did he have more letters?" Digger asked. "I hope they didn't get wet."

"Just that small diary we talked about in the wee hours this morning."

Digger stopped with her hand on the electric can opener. Ragdoll swatted her. "And if it's as wet as the passport Montgomery found, it's mostly gone."

"He had it in a Ziploc bag, so if the seal held and it didn't actually fall in, it could still be in the backpack."

The whir of the can opener also attracted Bitsy. "You have your food." She emptied half of the can into Ragdoll's bowl and put it on the floor. "You said you didn't really read the diary, right?"

"I skimmed only a few pages. Nowadays diaries are huge. This was maybe three by four inches. Harder to slip into. I think he bought it in Europe, because it had a cloth cover. Well, I suppose most of them did in the 1940s…"

Digger interrupted him. "What did it say?"

"He didn't talk much about the war. They couldn't. Nothing any soldier wrote could mention troop numbers or where they were."

Digger held her tongue. She wished he'd get to the point.

"He talked about missing home, about high school. And about the farmhouse his family used to live in. He barely remembered it, but from a couple pictures and things his parents mentioned, he felt as if he'd lived there a long time. It sounded as if he was describing it for his girlfriend's benefit."

"That's lovely, but did it say anything that might have led Peter to come here?"

"I had just gotten to the theories Thaddeus and his brother Thomas had about whether their father had buried anything near the foundation of the house before the lake filled. Then Saturday dinner was over."

Digger looked out the window at the layer of colorful leaves that coated the lawn and the two large flower and vegetable gardens. "Did Thaddeus believe his father hid things?"

Marty came through the swinging door from the dining room. "Half-an-hour?" He kissed her cheek.

"Oh, I forgot. Sorry. I've been talking to Uncle Benjamin."

"I'll remember to set my phone alarm." He took two mugs from a cupboard, then noticed Digger's eyes swing from the table back to him. "Big conversation? Good morning, Benjamin."

"Tell him I'll reserve judgment."

"Uncle Benjamin already mentioned the diary that was in Peter's backpack."

Marty had been about to open the fridge, but instead he straightened and looked directly at Digger. "Too bad he didn't read it."

"You can tell him what I told you."

"He read a little. Remember, he said it wasn't Peter's, it was his great-grandfather's. From before he died, obviously."

Marty poured his coffee and a fresh one for Digger. "I'm no expert, but wouldn't the Army have sent that back to Thaddeus' parents? How did Peter get it? And who knows if it's legitimate?"

"It's the reporter in him. Asking questions even if there's no way you'll know the answers."

Digger smiled at Uncle Benjamin and repeated his point. "I'm going to assume Thaddeus gave it to Marta Durkin, later Schmidt. Remember, the letter told her to look in the woodshed?"

For the next ten seconds, Digger watched Marty process this information, figuring he'd reach the same conclusion she did. When she thought he had, she continued, "Peter Becker said he received some family history materials after his Grandmother Bridget died. The diary must've been part of it."

"And," Marty said, "he started looking for his great-grandfather's relatives. Maybe just to find them, but maybe because he wanted to come here to see if anything could still be buried in the lake."

Digger shrugged. "It's not impossible he'd want to look, given his affinity for jewelry that German newspaper talked about."

"What affinity?" Uncle Benjamin asked.

Digger looked to Marty. "You found it."

"An article in a German paper suggested he stole a valuable bracelet from a local jeweler."

Uncle Benjamin pondered that. *"Did he go to jail?"*

Digger repeated his question, and answered. "We didn't find anything about that, but it was late. We went to bed for a couple of hours."

"There's more in that diary. And maybe other info in one of his notebooks. You need to visit the sheriff today."

"He wants another look at the diary and anything else in the backpack."

"You'll have to go to Oakland," Marty said, "it won't be at the satellite office in Maple Grove."

She nodded. I want to see the pictures of the two men they brought in last week for being on the lake at night. Those two guys weren't playing scuba diving. I bet they were working with Peter."

"No blue ribbon, but still a good conclusion."

"Please don't interrupt." To Marty, she added, "I texted Sheriff Montgomery and he said no sign of Peter. He was going to tell Thelma about last night, and suggest that Maryann sit with her, if she wanted company."

"You have to work today?"

"Only part of the day. I'll go down to Oakland, then head to the office for a little while, and then go to some of the tourist areas to look for clients."

Marty grinned. "And some of those businesses could be near where the empty boat was discovered?"

DIGGER TEXTED HOLLY that she'd be in at nine-thirty that Monday morning, and headed for Oakland with Uncle Benjamin. "If you find the diary, try to hit the highlights. The sheriff or one of the deputies won't talk to me too long, probably. I'll have to leave."

"I know. We learned the hard way that I fade away if you leave me behind."

"More like if you don't pay attention," she shot back.

"You're supposed to be creative. Improvise, so you can drag out the time you're there."

Digger thought quietly for several minutes as she drove. She wanted to see the photos of the two men to compare them to Robert Thorn and the so-called Elmo. Sheriff Montgomery wouldn't understand why she hadn't thought the men who made Peter uncomfortable were the same two who'd gone onto the lake at night. But why would she?

Now, it seemed obvious to at least check. But, how? If Sheriff Montgomery had been with Peter in the library when the two men showed up, Montgomery wouldn't have thought Peter was in cahoots with them. Only that he seemed very ill at ease.

And he had been. But not, as it appeared at the time, because they were grungy or pestered him to go for beer. She now believed Peter had worked with them to look for the old Zorn farmhouse. Possibly had hired them to go into the lake. But how would he have found them? She hadn't heard about any ads for someone to "dive in the lake at night to look for sunken treasure."

"I smell rubber burning," Uncle Benjamin said.

"What? Oh." Digger outlined what she'd been thinking.

"I've known Roger Montgomery a long time. He can spot a liar from across the bar at the VFW. He won't like what you tell him, but he'll know you weren't hiding anything from him earlier."

"I could be wrong. They could be very different men."

AFTER DIGGER WAITED FOR a few minutes, a receptionist at the Oakland law enforcement building escorted her to the sheriff's office.

He looked up from a folder on his desk. "Got a lot going on here today, Digger. You have news about the Becker guy?"

"Not exactly, but maybe a couple people who came up to him in the library when he was there with Thelma and me." She explained about Robert Thorn and his cohort, supposedly named Elmer but called Elmo. "Could they have been the men picked up for scuba diving on the lake a few nights ago?"

As Digger had anticipated, Sheriff Montgomery was irritated. He slid copies of the two mug shots across the desk to her, then sat behind the large desk turning redder by the second.

"They...could be the same," Digger said.

For almost a minute while the sheriff spouted at her, Uncle Benjamin stood behind him, mimicking gestures and alternately frowning or bringing his hands to his cheeks as if shocked.

Digger had a hard time focusing on Montgomery.

"You think this is funny?" he asked.

Uncle Benjamin waved at Digger and sped out the office door.

"No!" She started to say more, but he continued.

"If I had known that Peter Becker knew the dead man, I could've identified him by going to the motel and his family would already know he died."

Digger was tired of being scolded. "I don't know for sure if they were the same men. If you had published the photos of the two men you arrested on the lake last week, I might've recognized Robert Thorn." Digger wasn't totally sure of that. The two mug shots weren't a great comparison. For one thing, Thorn had had a beard in the photo, and when she saw him in the library, he'd been clean-shaven. And she hadn't seen him for more than ten years.

"First, we don't put out photos for every dumb thing people in Garrett County do. Second, I don't need you telling me how to do my job."

Uncle Benjamin zoomed into the room, gave her a thumbs up, and left through a different wall.

Digger swallowed. She didn't want to get thrown out of the sheriff's office. "I'm sorry. But, uh, no one recognized the body from those mug shots?"

He glowered at her. "Faces that have been in the lake a few hours look different. Especially if the fish found them first."

Digger's stomach almost heaved. "Sooo, what was his name? At the library, he said it was Elmer. Or Robert Thorn called him that."

"Fingerprints the ME got from the body in the lake ID'd him as Elmer Waterman. He grew up somewhere in Garrett County, but at some point moved closer to Cumberland. We haven't located family yet, but we will."

"Why were his fingerprints on file somewhere?"

Montgomery stood. "Digger, I have a busy day ahead."

She stood, too. "But he must've done something."

Montgomery pointed toward the door to his office. "Petty theft. Go away."

At the door, she turned. "Is Maryann going to spend time with Thelma today?"

"She made the offer."

IN HER CAR, DIGGER adjusted her seat and pretended to look through her purse. Where was Uncle Benjamin? Her Jeep was in a visitor parking space just outside the entrance. She didn't want to move it. As the crow flies, or the ghost floats, Uncle Benjamin could be anywhere from twenty to 100 yards from her.

How much farther away could she be before he started to fade? Or maybe her intent had something to do with it. She wouldn't drive away without him.

A car beeped behind her. A gentle beep, sort of an "are you leaving or what?" beep. Digger looked in her rearview mirror, waved, and put the Jeep in reverse. As she began moving, Uncle Benjamin came in through the front passenger window.

She stepped on the brakes, hard. "Jeezy peezy!"

"Sorry. Thought you forgot me."

Digger waved at the driver of an old Chrysler and pulled into the street. "What took you so long? Did you find out anything?

And don't ever make faces at me again when I'm trying to talk to someone!"

"It doesn't matter how clean water is, you have to scrub out a bag or it starts to stink after a couple days."

"I meant about what Peter had in his backpack. Wait, you could smell it?"

"I think I did get some rank sniffs. You think I'll be able to smell coffee now?"

"You can check back at the office. What did you find out?"

"Like I thought, that little diary was more like…ruminations about this Thaddeus' life before the war. He probably meant to write it for his honey-bunch, but my guess is it also made him feel better. He talked a few times about how close he was to one brother, Thomas, I think. How much he wanted to be home."

"Was he scared? Could you tell?"

"Couldn't tell about scared, but his writing got sloppier near the end. Maybe he knew something was about to happen and was in a hurry. Don't think the Allies thought the Germans would make as big a push as they did that December, but the guys must have suspected something."

Digger wanted specifics about what Thaddeus Zorn wrote that gave Peter ideas about coming to America to search for riches. "Did he mention the farmhouse that's in the lake?"

"A fair bit. He had one of those little circular push toys, you know, with the wood balls in them? Made a lot of racket and he liked to run down the big farmhouse kitchen with it."

"Uh huh."

"He didn't have a lot of memories from living there, but he said when he got home, he wanted to learn how to dive into the lake to look at the old house. Sounded as if he did it a couple times before he left for the War."

"Really? Did he see much?"

"At that time, guess it was late 1930s or early 1940s, the house was still largely intact. No windows, front porch collapsed. But there were still two floors. Even if the water was clear, he would have only been down a few feet."

"Did he mention actually poking around near the chimney? At the foundation?"

"Couldn't stay down long enough. Talked about showing this Marta the lake, and teased her about learning to swim so she could dive for treasure."

Digger wanted more specifics. "Did he say he thought there were items buried near the foundation?"

"He kinda made fun of himself. Said when he was little, he and Thomas pretended they were pirates going after gold doubloons. He said he heard his father buried some gold coins in little boxes, and that his dad got in a lot of trouble for including a couple pieces of his mother's jewelry. He never really said why his father did such a boneheaded thing."

"One of the letters Thelma's brother sent her said their father was hiding them until they got settled in Oakland. He thought their new house might attract burglars."

"Yep, a bonehead."

"What else was in the backpack?"

"Should've told you this first. Peter had a notebook he used a lot. Some family information, but mostly logistics about this trip. Including a couple loose pages he printed about – get this – places to stay on the lake. Where you could rent a boat."

Digger felt excited. "Did he do it?"

"Can't tell. No receipts or anything."

"Anything about the two guys he said bothered him?"

A few pages near the end he wrote their names and a phone number."

"How in the heck did he make contact with them? It's not like you could advertise in the paper."

"You and Holly do everything on the computer. Must've done one of those Google search things."

"Hey, was his computer in there?"

"No. Change of clothes, a paperback in German, granola bars, pens. No computer."

Digger could see the image of Peter walking into the Cumberland train station with his backpack, pulling a suitcase on wheels. Wherever the computer was, would it tell them a lot?

CHAPTER TWELVE

BEFORE DIGGER AND UNCLE BENJAMIN got to You Think, We Design at nine-thirty, Digger remembered to tell him more about the news articles Marty found in the wee hours of the morning. Uncle Benjamin was inclined to think the shoplifter had to be a different Peter Becker. Digger doubted it, but let him think what he wanted. She'd let the facts convince him later.

In the office, she absently made coffee while Uncle Benjamin peered out the picture window that overlooked the street. *"I hardly see anyone I know walking down the road anymore."*

Digger didn't want to tell him that most of the people he used to know were in the city cemetery. "You still know Thelma."

Uncle Benjamin's shoulders sagged. *"Can't talk to her. Wish I could help her. I had started to like that Peter."*

Digger sat her coffee on her desk, stared at the office phone for a moment, and picked up the receiver.

Thelma's nose sounded congested when she answered with a tremulous hello.

"Good morning, Thelma. I would have called earlier but wasn't sure what would be too early."

Thelma interrupted. "Has Peter called you?"

"I'm sorry, no. I wanted to tell you I hope the sheriff has good luck locating him."

Her tone sounded accusatory. "I don't understand any of this! You were going to drop him at the train station. He must have landed in Germany by now."

"I'd call that extreme optimism. Or more like gullibility," Uncle Benjamin said.

"I would like to think so, but did the sheriff tell you he has Peter's passport? His very wet passport."

Silence for several seconds. "No. What does it mean?"

"I'm not sure. It could be anything from a pickpocket to...I don't know. It sounds as if Peter may have come back to Garrett County."

Thelma almost whispered. "And drowned?"

"I haven't heard that. Apparently, someone else drowned in the lake last night or early this morning. It seems if Peter had, the sheriff would know by now."

She was silent, then said, "I hate not knowing."

"Sheriff Montgomery will work hard to figure it out." Digger took a quick sip of coffee to fortify herself. "Sheriff Montgomery said his grandmother might visit you later."

Thelma sighed. "Maryann has already called. She found a number of photos of Oakland from her childhood and high school years. I suppose it will be nice to see them."

"Marty and I are both going to keep our ears open today. You can call me anytime."

Thelma's voice grew resolute. "I want to know anything, Digger, even if it is bad news."

"I understand," Digger said, and hung up.

"Roger Montgomery would call her before you," Uncle Benjamin said.

Holly came up the stairs quickly and stood in the doorway regarding Digger. "I'd say a regular hello, Digger, but on the radio, they mentioned an empty boat the DNR Police found floating in Deep Creek Lake. Did Marty hear anything?"

Glumly, Digger added, "You don't want to know about the body they found there later?"

"What! Who was it? Wait, I need coffee first." She put her purse on her desk and headed for the coffee pot.

"Marty's heard a name." She didn't say she had gotten it directly from the sheriff. "I didn't know the man. Elmer Waterman." She didn't mention Robert Thorn might have been there, too.

Holly frowned. "I haven't heard the name either."

"At least it wasn't Peter Becker." As soon as she said that Digger could have slapped herself.

"But why would they even think it could be Peter?"

"Because his backpack was dangling halfway off the boat."

Holly sat her mug on her desk hard enough that drops of coffee splashed around it. "Who told you that?"

"Sheriff Montgomery was on my front porch at three AM. I told him I'd dropped Peter at the train station in Cumberland in the early afternoon."

Holly thought about that for several seconds. "So, he comes by rather than calls?"

Uncle Benjamin sat on the kitchenette counter, trying to smell the coffee. *"I wondered about that, too."*

"I suppose if Peter had been at the Ancestral Sanctuary, Montgomery would have had a lot of questions for him," Digger said.

"Gee, like how'd his backpack get in a boat or why did he leave it there?"

"And probably whether he could walk on water, since the boat was empty." Digger tried to fake a smile but didn't totally succeed. "First step to being a good sleuth is asking pertinent questions."

Holly snorted. "I'd like answers, I'm not willing to hunt for them." She studied Digger's face. "Where was it? What kind of boat?"

"Near Thayerville. Just one of those small, aluminum fishing boats."

Uncle Benjamin sat on Holly's desk. *"It couldn't have been put in the water there. Lots of security cameras near those hotels and their docks."*

"It could have entered the lake some distance from Thayerville. Someplace without a lot of traffic," Digger said.

"Or a lot of people on the lake after dark," Holly said. "Do you think Peter was with the man who died?"

"I assumed he was with them, but I can't be sure, I guess."

"You know what they say about making assumptions? Makes an ass out of you and me."

"Why would he be with them?"

"They knew him from the Oakland Motel, and they came into the library while Thelma and I were there with Peter. He seemed uncomfortable around them. One of those men was Elmer

Waterman, the guy who died. It just seems that if he's dead and Peter's missing…" Her voice trailed off and she tilted her head back and rolled her shoulders. "I'm tired, and there've been a lot of…frustrations the last twelve hours."

"And worry, too," Holly said. "I'm surprised you came in."

Digger grinned. "This is my sane place." She grew serious. "I need to call the School Board office to talk about doing next year's ornate attendance calendar so it's ready by Christmas. Then I'm going to head down to the lake."

"Going boating?"

"Funny. I can go to small businesses and leave our business flyer, and maybe I'll hear people talk about hearing noise on the lake in the middle of the night. Or whatever."

Holly nodded. "I'll go with you. We can take two cars and work near each other, but separately enough that we'll hear different things."

Caught off guard, Digger stared at her.

"Unless you don't want…"

"I'd love it," Digger said. She didn't add that it would be good because between her conversation with Franklin about the Ancestral Sanctuary and Peter's disappearance, she felt on edge. "The company would be great and four ears are better than two."

Uncle Benjamin almost pouted. *"How come you never tell me that?"*

DIGGER FOLLOWED HOLLY down Meadow Mountain onto Route 219, heading up to Thayerville. Fall colors were in full bloom and the bright blue sky lightened her mood. She shouldn't waste time thinking about Peter Becker. Really, he was no one to her. In fact, he had taken advantage of her good nature and wormed his way into her life.

Of course, he meant a lot to Thelma, even though she'd only known him a short time. He represented a link to the oldest brother she never knew. It probably meant even more now, since she'd lost her last sibling.

After she and Holly visited businesses in Thayerville, she would put anything related to Peter Becker out of her mind. She couldn't control what happened to him.

Uncle Benjamin interrupted her thoughts. *"That diary Thelma's brother wrote said he'd seen their house underwater. But that was in about 1940. Eighty years ago. All there'd be now would be a pile of soggy lumber. If that.*

"True. But I think one of her brother Thomas' letters mentioned their father buried the little boxes near the chimney, with stones or bricks over them. There'd at least be a pile of bricks."

"I suppose. It isn't salt water, which would break down the bricks faster."

Digger pulled into the parking lot of Coffee and More, where they planned to bolster their caffeine levels, plan what businesses to visit, and call Marty to see what he'd learned before they wandered around hotels and businesses. The coffee shop had been built since the pandemic, so it had two pick-up windows for drive-by orders and only a small seating area.

They walked in together and Uncle Benjamin immediately began to follow baristas as they poured different brands of coffee. From the disappointed look on his face, he still couldn't smell it.

They got their coffee – a latte for Digger since it was her third cup – and took a table away from other customers. Marty answered on the third ring and Digger told him where they were.

"How come you didn't invite me to the lake?"

"At least she didn't tell you not to butt in. Or one of them didn't tell you that," Uncle Benjamin groused.

Digger smiled at Holly. "We need you pounding the pavements in Oakland. At our office, I told Holly the men Peter saw in the library could be the same two who were arrested last week. Are you picking up anything at the hospital or sheriff's office?"

"DNR Police are asking people near Thayerville if they heard anything. One guy said he couldn't sleep and heard oars in the water. He used binoculars and could see three people in a small boat, about 100 yards out from that big resort hotel." He chuckled. "He said he figured they were fishing so he didn't call anyone, and the police officer was mad he didn't call. Guy hung up on them."

"How do you know that?" Holly asked.

"Deputy Collins thought it was funny and told me."

"That's the general area they found the boat in," Digger said. "They must've dropped anchor, or it would have drifted farther."

"I got that much out of Collins, then he clammed up," Marty said.

Holly looked at notes she'd made as they talked. "We know the boat was anchored, but we need to find out if they rented it."

"The sheriff said he didn't think so," Digger said.

Holly moved the crust of the croissant on her plate. "But if you think Peter was with those two guys who were scuba diving last week, the sheriff would have to know something about that boat."

"You should come with me more often," Digger grinned.

Uncle Benjamin had donned a 1920s striped, men's bathing suit and spoke from where he sat on a railing that overlooked the lake. *"Find out if Marty saw the mugshot pictures of the two scuba diver wannabes."*

Digger told Marty she'd seen the mugshot photos and asked if he'd seen them.

"It's public information but it wasn't on the sheriff's website. After I called, they put it on, but didn't link those guys to the empty boat or the dead guy."

"I suppose they'd need to know more to do that," Holly said.

"Probably. The sheriff called to tell me to watch myself. Like, be careful, not telling me to back off entirely."

"Probably means they think the other guy didn't drown when he was skinny dipping," Uncle Benjamin said.

"You think Sheriff Montgomery thinks Elmer Waterman was murdered?" Digger asked.

"Ugh," Holly said.

"Our ME's office is working with DNR, since the body was in the lake. But no one at the ME's office is telling me anything, so I'd think they're leaning that way. Don't know for sure."

Holly frowned and stirred sugar into her coffee very fast. "We can't do more than listen and pass out our marketing info at businesses."

Digger thought her partner was having second thoughts about being there. "I'll talk to boat rental places and the big hotels right on the lake. Why don't you do the gift shops on the other side of Route 219 and that convenience store. Then we can regroup."

"There are a few small, older motels," Marty said. "That's more like where they would have stayed. At least the two divers. Peter didn't have a rental car, did he?"

"He turned it in before he came to stay at the Ancestral Sanctuary."

"He had to rent another car," Holly said.

"Or someone picked him up and drove him back to Deep Creek Lake. He had the money to rent one, didn't he?" Marty asked.

"He said he was conserving funds," Digger said, "but not that he was really strapped."

"We can do the small motels together," Holly said. "But in one car. There's hardly any parking at those places."

DIGGER PULLED INTO the parking lot of the large resort hotel that faced the water. In the summer, masses of flowers cascaded down a small hill toward the hotel's large dock. Even now red and yellow mums still withstood the chilly nights.

In the spacious lobby, she studied the few people lounging near the hearth. The deep burgundy couches looked more like something you'd find in a law office, but they went well with the arching wood beams.

No sign of Peter, not that she'd expected to see him. She headed for the front desk and pulled a You Think, We Design brochure from the folder she carried.

Patrick the desk clerk, according to the name on his badge, looked all of twenty and very eager to please. "What can I do for you?"

Digger smiled brightly and went into her spiel, closing with, "You probably don't decide on advertising or brochures, but maybe you can direct me to the person who does."

He nodded, slowly. "That's Ms. Burroughs, but she isn't in this morning. You can leave a copy of the flyer and your card. She always calls people back."

Digger wrote her mobile number on the back of the card. "I bet everybody's talking about the body found in the lake near here."

Patrick lowered his voice. "We aren't supposed to talk about it with guests, but you aren't staying here. So, yeah, we all wonder who it was."

Digger didn't volunteer any names.

He leaned across the desk and lowered his voice, "We heard an empty boat was near there, but it didn't have fishing rods or bait."

"Must not have had life vests, either," she said.

Uncle Benjamin stood behind the counter, with Patrick, and sported a nametag that said Boss. *"Sounds like they wanted to find what they were looking for last week."*

Patrick shrugged and almost whispered. "I didn't hear if there were any in the boat. They did have snorkeling gear. You can't see anything at night."

"Snorkeling gear, not scuba diving equipment?"

When Patrick gave her a questioning look, Digger added, "I get them mixed up."

He shrugged. "I think the deputy who came by this morning said snorkeling. He was trying to find out if we rented snorkeling masks and fins here." He frowned. "I don't think I was supposed to say that."

Digger put a finger on her lips. "I didn't hear you." She pointed at the brochure on the counter. "I look forward to hearing from Ms. Burroughs."

All smiles again, he handed her one of the hotel's expensive-looking brochures and suggested she give it to friends.

Uncle Benjamin joined Digger as she left. *"If he had a guest book, I could have looked at names, but I guess it's all on the computer."*

Digger nodded as she walked slowly to her car. She couldn't exactly ask if a water-logged guest had come through the lobby at two or three AM.

CHAPTER THIRTEEN

The hotel had its own docks, but Digger knew those were for guests' boats and pleasure craft the hotel rented to guests. Without a room key, people couldn't rent the hotel's boats. She doubted Peter would've paid those rates, and Robert Thorn didn't look as if he had that kind of money.

A commercial boat rental place was only a few hundred yards from the hotel, so she headed there. Her story would be that she had friends coming into town and she wanted to get price information.

The boat rental business owner's lined skin said he spent a lot of time without sunscreen. He greeted her on the dock, listened to her question about renting, and eyed her with something close to suspicion. "You a reporter, are you?"

"Me? No. Why would you ask that? Oh." She held up the small notebook she carried just to have something in her hands. "I'm writing down prices so I can compare them."

"Huh. Well, I'm not the cheapest, but you shouldn't rent a boat or a car from places with rock-bottom prices." He pulled from a pocket of his cargo pants a half-page flyer that listed hourly and all-day prices for kayaks, canoes, and jon boats. No sailboats.

As she took it, Digger saw Uncle Benjamin floating out of the small building, almost a shack, where the dock manager probably kept records. He now wore a blue blazer, white pants, and brimmed hat of a boat captain.

Surprised, she dropped the price list. "Butterfingers."

With more than a tinge of impatience, the man said, "No problem."

Digger glanced at the paper as if she really cared what it said, and looked at him again. "Why did you ask me if I'm a reporter?"

He tilted his head behind him, in the direction of the water. "Some poor fella drowned out there."

"That's awful! Did you rent them the boat?"

"Nah. Happened at night. I don't rent anything overnight."

"I thought people couldn't be on the lake at night."

"Yep. I figure he didn't want to spend money on a license." His eyes narrowed. "I gotta see a state boating license before you rent."

Digger smiled. "One of my friends has one. I should probably take the training."

"First rule, never take off your life vest. I don't care how long you been boating."

Digger thanked him for the advice and walked across the slightly swaying dock and up the few steps toward the parking area. All she had really learned was that people were aware of an apparent drowning. No one mentioned a crime, much less murder.

She would have thought the man would more about what had happened, maybe question whether it was an accidental drowning. Apparently, not.

Uncle Benjamin joined her as she neared her car. *"He has lists of people he's rented to, sloppy handwriting. I didn't see Peter Becker's name, or the other two."*

"Mmm." With her mouth mostly closed, Digger asked, "Those two didn't strike me as the types to ask permission to use a boat, much less pay."

"Ah, midnight acquisitions, you mean?" Uncle Benjamin switched to a trench coat and held a magnifying glass.

Digger shook her head slightly as she popped the locks on her Jeep. "You're changing outfits a lot today."

At the car next to hers, a man had been looking in his trunk and he stood up. "Were you talking to me?"

Uncle Benjamin laughed and dove into her back seat.

"Sorry, to myself. My outfit's too hot for the day." She did wish she'd worn capris instead of long pants.

Uninterested, the man resumed searching his trunk.

DIGGER HAD SIMILAR RESULTS at the Crafty Crew boat rental. She had a hard time concentrating because Uncle

Benjamin kept talking to himself about whether ghosts could swim. He wasn't inclined to just try it.

As they went back to her car, something occurred to Digger and she slapped herself on the forehead. She glanced around; they were alone in the small lot. "I just realized, if you could swim, you could go down to see what's left of the Zorn house."

He shrugged. *"Maybe, but I couldn't dig around the foundation to look for those tin boxes."*

She popped the car's locks and got in. "True, and I have no intention of diving thirty feet or more to look. Somebody around here must do that. You know, for a fee."

"Ask at one of the hotels to see if anyone gives lessons."

"Good idea." She sat in the car and called Holly. "I haven't found much. You want to meet at the Good Rest Inn, next to the gas station?"

"Yeah. I drove by it. There's enough room for both our cars in their lot."

Digger beat her there, but found more cars than Holly seemed to have expected. She parked at the far end of the lot, next to the last unit. She tried not to turn her nose up at the faded dark blue window trim or scuffed doors that looked as if they'd been bumped by hundreds of pieces of luggage.

"Guess they don't have a big budget for upkeep," Uncle Benjamin said. He stuck his head through a curtained window and quickly pulled it out. *"Whoa."*

Quietly, Digger said, "That'll teach you to mind your own business."

She and Holly met at the office, which featured pine paneling and was as cramped as every motel office built in the 1950s or thereabouts. Digger wondered how it had survived this long.

Holly introduced them to the front desk clerk, whose nameplate claimed she was Monica. "We're from Maple Grove, and thought we'd leave a brochure about our graphics design business."

Digger had expected a bored reaction, but Monica smiled broadly. "I'm studying computer aided design at Garrett College. My parents keep asking me what I'm going to do besides make TikTok videos." She took the brochure.

Holly matched the smile. "Nowadays, lots of people can use software like Photoshop or Canva, but most businesses want professional-looking brochures or annual reports; even TikTok videos. But they don't want to keep designers on staff."

Digger jumped in. "Holly and I can attest to that. We used to work for the Western Maryland Advertising Agency. They laid off a bunch of us about eighteen months ago."

Holly nodded. "You could find a job with a company, but there is a lot of freelance work, too. Like we do."

Monica studied the brochure and then looked up. "I bet you do good work, but," she scrunched her nose for a second, "the people who own this place don't usually pay for advertising. Rates are cheap enough that people seem to find us."

Digger had not noticed the large ledger book of guest names until Uncle Benjamin dove into it. She turned back to Monica. "We hear that a lot. But even if they don't do it regularly, they might want to sometime, and they'll have our brochure."

Monica looked at Holly, who held several, as well as their business cards. "Can you give me a couple? I want to show them to some of the kids in my class."

They both said, "Sure," glanced at each other and laughed.

Monica studied them. "You guys are really good friends, right?"

Digger nodded and Holly simply said yes.

Monica hesitated. "Like best friends?"

It seemed an odd question, but Holly said, "On our best days."

Monica nodded, very serious. "I've never known best friends who are black and white."

Holly didn't miss a beat. "It's not so common here, but if you head over to Frostburg after you get your two-year degree, you'll see more of it."

"Huh. That makes sense, I guess." She tapped a brochure on the counter. "I'll give these to Mrs. Dundy."

"Sounds good," Digger said.

Monica had stayed seated, and it would be awkward to reach over the counter to shake hands, so they said goodbye and walked out.

Digger nodded to her car, which was farther from the office, and spoke softly. "I was so surprised by her point at the end I didn't ask about the guys staying here."

Holly glanced at her car. "Ditto. She was friendly. She probably would have told us."

Uncle Benjamin appeared next to Holly, and Digger started. *"Robert Thorn was in that guest book. And he had a boat trailer. They have to list it when they register."*

She acknowledged him with a nod. "I agree. But if we go back in now, it won't be a very natural conversation."

"Yep." Holly started for her car, which was across from the office. "I don't know, Digger. I liked coming up here to pass out brochures, but I don't think I'm cut out for detecting stuff."

"Takes a kind of warped mind." Uncle Benjamin sped toward Digger's Jeep.

Digger grinned. "It does require persistence and…"

"Devious thinking. You want to get a sandwich at the Spicy Crab?"

"Good idea." She kissed Holly on the cheek. "Meet you there."

Digger looked for Uncle Benjamin as she trudged to her Jeep. As she beeped the key fob, he popped out of the brush on the side of the motel. *"There's a rusty-looking boat trailer back there."*

Digger got in the Jeep. "Given the looks of this place, it could've been there for years."

"There's mud on the tires, so no. Write this down."

"What?"

"Do it before I forget, okay?"

Digger took a pen from her cup holder and opened the notebook she'd left on the seat. "What?"

"CV0000," Uncle Benjamin said.

"Is that a password you want me to use for my family history computer files?"

"Trailer license. Can Marty check those things?"

"I don't think so. I can just hear the sheriff if I call him about this."

"Tell Marty to pretend he found it."

"Let me think about it."

He folded his arms and sat straighter in the Jeep's passenger seat. *"I come up with a good clue and you ignore me."*

Digger grinned. "Okay, I'll talk to Marty and one of us will call."

She backed out of the parking space and headed to meet Holly at the Spicy Crab, one of the older restaurants that sat a block back from the lake. Prices for food and lodging went down in proportion to distance from the shoreline. Plus, she liked the crabcake sandwiches. Even though they were mostly breading.

To make sure her entire Jeep was in the shade, Digger backed into a space that sat at the foot of a small rise, with a mix of poplar and maples providing shade. Even though the fall temperature wouldn't go above sixty, the bright day would make the pavement hot and her Jeep warm and stuffy. She put each window down several inches.

Holly pulled in close to the Spicy Crab entrance and waved to her. Digger waved back before she took her purse from the car. Because the window was down, she didn't lock it. Anyone could reach in. but no one would.

Holly pulled open the glass door for them. "Did you hear from Marty? He must have found out something."

Digger shook her head. "I thought we'd call him from here. Unless it's really noisy." She elbowed Holly lightly. "Thought you didn't want to look for info."

"I don't mind hearing what you find out."

They seated themselves at a table beneath a huge poster of a bucket of crabs with a sweating bottle of beer next to it.

Digger's phone vibrated. She nodded to Holly and quietly answered. "Marty. What's up?"

"Nothing that you couldn't read in the Pittsburgh or Cumberland papers tomorrow." She rolled her eyes toward Holly. "I'm sorry you don't publish every day. Pretend I don't want to wait for a major daily. What did you find out?" She couldn't put the phone on speaker, so she held it toward Holly.

"Because there were three reporters in the waiting area in the Oakland office, Sheriff Montgomery came out and said that the official cause of death was drowning, but he couldn't talk to us about 'any contusions' the man might have had on his head."

"So, he's really saying someone hit the guy?"

"Not yet. He did say he contacted this Elmer Waterman's family outside of Cumberland. Because he got hold of some family he was willing to tell us the name."

"You wouldn't learn to steer a boat there," Holly said.

"The phrase is pilot a boat," Marty said, genially. "And no, you probably wouldn't. Did you find out where they rented one?"

"No," Digger said. "I suppose if one of the other two men owned it, the boat could have already been at the smaller dock, not near the hotel. Then they could have snuck into it at night."

"Or put it in at the shore, where it isn't too rocky," Uncle Benjamin said.

"But why take risks like that?" Holly asked. "Just to fish?"

Fishing for something that wasn't theirs, Digger thought. She had to be careful. Holly knew nothing of Peter's background or the diary he had brought with him from Germany. "From hearing Thelma talk to Peter, the spot where the empty boat was could be near her family's old farmhouse, from before the land was flooded for the lake. Peter's…really into knowing more about his newfound family."

Holly waved a hand to dismiss the idea. "The only way to see anything in the lake at night would be to have some special diving equipment and lights. And if they did see the house, it would be in pieces. What would be the point? They weren't going to find family heirlooms."

Marty said, "You wouldn't think so."

DIGGER AND HOLLY headed for the restaurant parking lot. "I'm glad you came." Digger grinned. "I really did get ideas for a couple of clients."

Holly gave a short laugh. "It's a good thing, because we didn't get any information on your friend or that boat." They stopped near Holly's car. "Remember how we had the idea for a standard menu design for restaurants in Maple Grove?"

"Your idea," Digger said. "A good one."

"You ended up designing some, too. I was thinking we could do something like that for flyers for B&Bs. They'd have a similar look, but be distinct."

"Or put four on a page, and suggest they join together to do a quarter page each in the *Maple Grove News*. We might get our foot in the door with a less expensive ad."

"That's good," Holly said. "We can talk tomorrow. This fresh air wore me out."

Digger grinned. "We're a good team."

"We are. Go home and walk your dog."

Digger moved toward her Jeep, but stopped. She juggled the to-go box with leftover hushpuppies and half of a brownie and pretended to take a call, but was actually calling Marty.

"Miss me?" he asked.

"Of course. But our friend also spotted a small boat trailer that looked partially hidden in the brush behind Good Rest Inn."

"Jeez. You didn't go to that place, did you?"

"It wasn't so bad. Uncle Benjamin said the tires on the trailer were muddy, so someone must have used it recently."

Marty was silent for several seconds. "But it would have been wherever they put the boat in, not at the motel."

Uncle Benjamin had been listening. *"Not if they didn't want it sitting by the shore or a dock. They could've put the boat in or near the spot where they were going to go in and then taken the trailer back."*

"You still there?" Marty asked.

"I was listening to my muse." She repeated what Uncle Benjamin had said. "I have the license. Maybe you could tell Montgomery you found it and ask him to check it."

"I suppose. I'll have to drive up there so I can see it and tell him where it is. He knows I've been down here all day."

"Tell him to snap to it."

"Uncle Benjamin wants you to hurry. He's proud he found a clue."

Marty laughed. "Tell him he'll probably crack the case."

Digger hung up and glanced around the peaceful setting, wishing their office sat next to the lake. This time of year, anyway. In summer, the hordes of people in flip flops and wet bathing suits would crowd her space.

Digger walked to her car at its spot under the nearby tree. She glanced toward the restaurant but didn't see Uncle Benjamin. He must have found a conversation he wanted to overhear. Maybe about the untended boat and the dead man.

She mentally slapped herself. She needed to stop thinking about Peter Becker. Beyond not wanting Thelma to be hurt, he was nothing to her. A tourist with sticky fingers who wheedled his way into her good nature.

She unlocked the car and slid behind the steering wheel.

The voice from the back seat made her drop her keys before they were all the way into the ignition.

"It is me, Peter. Please do not say you found me. I need to hide."

CHAPTER FOURTEEN

DIGGER DROPPED HER KEYS on the floor mat and glanced quickly toward Holly's car. Her partner had just pulled out of the lot. She honked but Holly didn't hear her and kept going.

"Please, Digger. Give me a chance to explain."

Digger put the windows down and opened her car door. "I'll stand outside the car and listen to you. Did you know a man died last night?"

She exited the car and kept the driver's door open. To make it appear she had a reason for getting out, she popped the trunk.

Peter said nothing for several seconds. "I thought, I thought it could be, but I didn't know."

"So, you were in that boat on the lake in the middle of the night?"

He didn't respond.

Digger glanced toward the restaurant. "I need to call the sheriff."

"Wait, please! I am exhausted. And hungry,"

Digger still hadn't looked at him. She reached across the driver's seat, grabbed the to-go box, and put it through the open back seat window. Peter was in something close to a fetal position on the floor behind the driver's seat.

He sat up and reached for the box, but didn't sit on the seat itself. His usually carefully styled hair stood up in places, having clearly been wet and dried without benefit of a comb. His wrinkled clothes looked as if they had been retrieved from a laundry basket.

Digger stood back while he ate the two hushpuppies. There could be no good reason for him to be on the lake or not immediately seek help if he had managed to crawl out of it after some kind of accident. What was he hiding?

He coughed and sputtered. "Do you have any water?"

"Half a bottle. It's warm." She retrieved it from the front seat cupholder and passed it through the window. She glanced around, thinking her behavior would look odd if anyone paid attention to her.

"Take your drink and talk."

He gulped all the water in a matter of seconds and then leaned against the still-closed car door, his back to her. Digger wished she could see his face as he talked.

"I, did not…I should have told you." He stopped.

"I think there's a lot you didn't tell me. Or Thelma. Keep talking."

"Thelma. She will hate me."

"Keep talking."

"I did find her through the DNA. I wanted to meet anyone from my great-grandfather's family. You see, I had, I had something he left for my great-grandmother, when he…before he died."

"The little diary? Your backpack didn't fall all the way out of the boat."

He sat up straight and turned to face her. "It did not? So, my passport is also found?"

Digger took in his flushed cheeks and tired eyes. "Very wet. I don't care about your passport just now. What in the heck were you doing in a boat at night, and who was with you?"

"Two men. You said someone died?"

Digger spoke sharply. "You must know someone died. Otherwise, you wouldn't be sneaking around. You would have called for help. For God's sake, I left you at the train station in Cumberland!"

From near the back entrance of the Spicy Crab, someone called. "You okay over there?"

Digger cursed inwardly and smiled at two women who stood near the restaurant steps. "Yes." She tapped her ear as if she had a Bluetooth device in it. "Just talking to a friend who's being annoying."

They relaxed and one called, "I know that routine." The other one elbowed her gently and they walked into the restaurant.

Digger looked into her back seat. "You haven't told me anything I didn't know."

"If I could only come with you. Back to your house. I could maybe take a shower and…"

"And try to fool everyone with your phony family story? Maybe that wasn't even your DNA test result."

"It was. I promise. Please, Digger."

He certainly sounded plaintive enough, but there was no reason for her to believe anything Peter Decker said. She took her phone from the pocket of her slacks and pushed Marty's speed dial button.

"Please don't call the sheriff!"

Marty answered in a clipped tone. "I'm not quite halfway there. I didn't ask where you were."

"Still in the parking lot at the Spicy Crab. Found someone we've been looking for."

Marty waited a beat. "Are you talking about Peter?"

"Yep, in my back seat."

"Is that Franklin? He'll believe me," Peter said.

"I hear him. You call the sheriff?"

Digger glanced around the parking lot. "Nope."

"Are you asking me to call Montgomery."

"Yep."

"Why are you being so terse?" Marty asked.

"I'm not sure what I'm dealing with."

"He isn't armed, is he?"

"I don't think so."

"I'm going to put you on hold and call. But I'll come back. I want you to keep the line open so I can hear what's going on."

Digger detected excitement in his tone. He wanted the story.

She shoved her phone back into a pocket. "Stay where you are. Marty's coming."

"Then can we go to your house?"

Uncle Benjamin was suddenly in the front seat of the car, peering into the back. *"Where did you find him? He looks like something a coyote dragged in."*

Digger wanted to ask him where the heck he had been when Peter almost gave her a heart attack. Instead, she ignored him and looked into the back seat. "Peter, I can't think of a single reason to trust you. In my place or anywhere else. Who was the man who died?"

He said nothing.

"Sheriff Montgomery made a name public. He said the guy was from outside Cumberland. How did you meet him?"

Uncle Benjamin floated into the back and sat on the console between the front seats. *"The guy wasn't honest before. He won't be now."*

Still no comment from the back seat.

"You want a lot from me, but you aren't telling me anything."

"He is, was, someone I met here."

"You didn't just 'meet' him. You were in a boat on the lake looking for anything that might have been buried in the foundation of the Zorn's old farmhouse."

His tone became more animated. "You know what is there?"

"Will you listen to yourself? Thelma welcomed you and you betrayed her."

"No, I, well before I met her, I would have taken what I found. After I knew her, I thought of giving her some of…whatever it would be."

"Hard to believe," Digger said.

His voice choked. "I should not have said that to the man. He became angry."

"Was that man Robert Thorn?"

Silence.

"Answer me, Peter."

"I found out that was his name. He called himself The Can Do Man."

"How did you meet him?" Digger asked.

Silence, then, "Through an advert." He used the British term, but didn't elaborate.

"An ad you placed somewhere, or one he had posted?"

He didn't reply. "What was Thorn angry about?" she asked.

"We were going to share…split if we found some things."

"Did he say he should get more?"

"I made a mistake. I suggested he and The Make Do Man get less. But also, me."

Digger figured the Make Do Man was Waterman. "While you were on the lake you suggested that? Smart."

Peter's tone was almost a whine. "It was for Thelma."

Digger thought for a moment. "You didn't want something for Thelma to come out of your so-called split? You wanted to divide things four ways instead of three?"

"Yes! It was her family's house. But the men. It was their boat. They said they did a lot of work. They said no."

Digger glanced toward the Spicy Crab to be sure no one was paying attention to them. Seeing no one, she turned back to the car window. "And you argued?"

"I said okay. We still split three ways. But then this Robert Thorn kept getting angrier. He had beers in the boat."

"So, you tried to hit one of them?" Digger asked.

Peter's head popped up from his crouched position. "I did not! I did not have a way to hit anyone. But the Make Do Man was behind me, and he, he shoved my shoulder. I said he should stop. When I turned back, this man you call Thorn had a shovel in his hand."

"You're saying he hit his partner?"

"I am saying he wanted to hit me. I stooped low. In American slang, I ducked. And then…" His voice choked. "Thorn missed me. The sharp edge of the shovel hit the Make Do Man instead."

Digger said nothing for several seconds. "And he fell into the water?"

Peter's voice dropped to a whisper. "And a lot of blood fell in the water, too."

Uncle Benjamin shook a fist at Peter. *"This jerk's going to tell you he jumped in to save that guy. He jumped in to save his own ass."*

There was no way for Digger to tell if Peter told the truth or simply added another lie to his list. "Then what? How did you get in the water?"

"This Thorn, he raised the shovel again. I jumped in the water. I tried to grab my backpack, but it caught on something. Then this Thorn, he threw the shovel at me. It missed my head and made a loud splash. I swam away, sometimes under the water."

Though Peter certainly looked as if he'd swum to shore and not eaten, it didn't mean she should accept what he said.

"Peter, I'm missing something. Why would you do this? Aside from taking advantage of Thelma, why go to such extremes for so-called treasure that might not even be hidden in the lake? Why not just…just get a job?"

He was silent for several seconds. "I tell you about my family. But they say they are no longer my family. I shamed them. So, I want to convince them I am successful. If I am rich, my mother will forgive me."

"For stealing that jewelry, you mean?"

His voice went up an octave. "This, this you know?"

"I wanted to find out more about you, when we thought you were missing. Internet searches, with the help of Google Translator."

He slumped against the car door. "I am so ashamed. You hate me now."

"I think that's the least…hey. You said your mother was worried, that's why you left."

"I had to make an excuse. The Can Do Man kept texting me. He said I still had to help him find the gold coins. Or he would tell Thelma I was a thief. When I still said no more looking, he said he would steal from her."

Digger stared at a squirrel sitting on a branch of the tree behind her car. He appeared to be sizing her up to see if she'd give him leftover food. Peter's story could be true, but how could you tell with someone who had lied so much?

As she thought about that, two vehicles turned into the Spicy Crab Parking lot. A Garrett County Sheriff SUV preceded Marty's Toyota. The SUV didn't have lights and sirens, but was a heavy vehicle.

Peter heard it and, still seated on the floor, peered out Digger's back window. "No! Do not say you see me."

Digger didn't want to hide Peter at the Ancestral Sanctuary. Out of loyalty to Thelma, she would have encouraged him to turn himself in. But he might well run away again. She stepped a few feet away from her Jeep and pointed to it as the SUV pulled up.

Deputy Keller, whom Digger didn't know well, got out of the SUV with a hand on his holster, leaving the car running. "Is he armed?"

"I've never seen him with a gun. Plus, he ended up in the lake last night, so if he had anything it seems to be gone."

Still holding his phone, Marty got out of his car and walked to within a few feet of Digger.

"Mister Becker, this is Deputy Keller from the Garrett County Sheriff's Department." He motioned that Digger should move back. "You two stand behind my vehicle." He raised his voice again. "I need you to exit the Jeep slowly, keeping your hands where I can see them."

Digger could hear Peter fumbling for the door handle. The door slowly opened. Since he'd been sitting, Peter's legs came out first. He pushed the door the rest of the way open, placed a hand on the arm rest, and stood unsteadily."

"Turn around slowly so I can be sure you're unarmed."

Peter did so. It gave Digger a chance to see how bad he looked. One pant leg had a three or four-inch tear, and his shirt had brown streaks that she hoped were mud from the lake bank as he climbed out. He wore only one shoe.

Deputy Keller took his hand off his holster and approached Peter. "Mr. Becker, you've been reported missing. You need to accompany me to Oakland to talk about where you've been and why your backpack was in an empty boat on the lake in the middle of the night."

Peter looked to Digger and then Marty. "Can I ride with one of my friends?"

Digger shook her head. "I'll let Thelma know you seem okay, but you need to ride to Oakland with the deputy."

"Thelma. Tell her...tell her I'm sorry."

"He should be," Uncle Benjamin said.

Marty squeezed Digger's elbow, but spoke to Peter. "When you get to Oakland, tell the sheriff if you need to see a doctor."

He nodded toward Peter's head. Digger realized that what she'd thought was disheveled hair was hair matted with blood.

"When I climbed out of the water, I slipped and hit my head on a rock. A pointed rock."

The deputy seemed to notice for the first time. "You can sit in the back of my vehicle without handcuffs if you can remain unemotional." The deputy opened the car's back door and Digger moved closer to Marty.

Peter walked stiffly to the SUV, winced as his shoeless foot found a large piece of gravel, and climbed in. The door locked automatically as the deputy shut it. Digger realized that the bulletproof glass that separated the deputy from his cargo was probably why he didn't cuff Peter. That and no arrest warrant had been issued as far as she knew.

Deputy Keller nodded to Marty. "Thanks for the call. Sheriff Montgomery said you can call him in an hour or so."

"Will do," he said. He and Digger backed up a few feet so the deputy could turn his vehicle around and head toward the parking lot exit.

Uncle Benjamin sped along beside them, peering in the back window at Peter.

Digger realized that about ten people had gathered on the Spicy Crab's back porch. One of the women who'd called to her earlier said, "Honey, you should have let me know to call the sheriff."

Digger shook her head and raised her voice some. "He's not dangerous, just confused." She turned her back on the group and regarded Marty. "Thanks."

"You okay?"

"Once I got over him surprising me from the floor of the back seat. I'm lucky I didn't wet my pants."

"I wouldn't have been able to offer you a ride home."

She grinned. "I'm fine to drive. I hope the sheriff gives you the story."

"He will. Plus," he held up his phone, "I got a couple of photos."

"I didn't see you do that."

They walked toward her Jeep and he shut its back door. "I didn't make the aiming obvious, and I pushed the button a bunch of times. There's usually one I can use."

"You better get it on your web page fast," Digger said. "Somebody on that porch probably took pictures."

"Jeez. I'll do that from my car, with just a caption. You better call Thelma."

"You going down to Oakland?"

"Yeah. If I sit in the lobby, the sheriff'll remember that he wants to talk to me first."

They stared at each other for a few seconds. "I believe I've told you my life was a lot less interesting before I met you." He leaned over and they hugged.

BEFORE SHE STARTED to drive home, Digger sat in her car for a minute. She needed to let Bitsy out to do his business, but before then, she should stop at Thelma's. Sheriff Montgomery would have called her, but that was no substitute for a visit from Benjamin Browning's niece.

"Why haven't you started the car?" Uncle Benjamin asked.

"Trying to figure out what to say to Thelma."

"Maryann is there, isn't she? There will be plenty of talk."

"You know what I mean."

Uncle Benjamin sighed, possibly the first time Digger had heard him do that. *"It'll be hard for her. Someone could say she barely knew him, but it's not like an acquaintance she met around town. Or even a neighbor."*

"Because he's family?"

"Because of what she imagined he could be as family. She lost her last brother and none of her nieces and nephews live near here. And they weren't close, anyway. Even if she didn't say it out loud, Thelma saw him as someone she'd always know. Someone who wanted to talk to her about the family she used to have."

Digger felt bereft at the prospect of becoming distant from Franklin. "That's…insightful." She started the car. "I'll stop at the grocery store in Maple Grove and get her some flowers.

CHAPTER FIFTEEN

WHEN SHE ARRIVED at Thelma's bungalow at about three-thirty, the blinds were drawn. "That's odd."

Uncle Benjamin floated through the front passenger window. *"I'll peek in there."*

Digger opened her door. "Remember what happened at the Good Rest Inn?"

"I didn't say I'd look in the bedroom." On the porch, he stuck his head through the front door.

"I hate it when he does that," Digger muttered.

He pulled his head out. *"Thelma's lying on the sofa with a compress on her head. Maryann's in a chair nearby, a book in her lap. Her cane's next to the chair. She better watch out or she'll trip on it."*

Digger walked up the steps, flowers in hand, and knocked softly.

Uncle Benjamin put his head through a window. *"Thelma waved at Maryann to answer it, so she's coming."*

"You don't need to stick your head through walls to give me a play-by-play."

"Humph." He floated through the door.

Maryann opened it an inch. She peered out and then opened it wider. "It's Digger. Come on in."

"Thanks." Digger touched Maryann's shoulder as she walked in. As Thelma moved, she added, "Don't sit up, Thelma."

Thelma had leaned on her elbow, but lay back down and placed the washcloth on her stomach. "I've been acting like a fainting wallflower."

Maryann took the washcloth. "No, you've had a shock and you've given friends permission to support you."

Digger sat at the foot of the couch. "Great way to put it."

Uncle Benjamin sat on the back of the couch, near Thelma's head. *"Remind her she's tough and she'll be okay."*

Digger looked at Thelma and nodded slightly. "This is all really disappointing."

Thelma closed her eyes briefly. "I really liked that young man. My own brother's great-grandson."

Digger glanced at Maryann. "Did the sher…your grandson come by?"

"He did," Maryann said. "He didn't seem to know much yet."

Digger realized she didn't know if he'd talked to Thelma after Peter had popped up in her car.

Maryann added. "He said Peter would be taken to Oakland, but he didn't know if he'd be arrested. He needed to talk to him."

Digger hesitated. "I know he's done some things he regrets, but I don't know that anything was illegal."

Thelma sat up, so Digger stood and moved to a chair. "What do you mean? Did you see him?"

Uncle Benjamin's tone was insistent. *"Tell her what I said!"*

Digger nodded, but didn't. "You probably heard he was in a boat on the lake last night and a man who was also in it drowned." She took a breath. "I was in Thayerville, with Holly today. When I came out of a restaurant, Peter had gotten into my back seat."

Thelma put a hand to her mouth.

"Where had he been?" Maryann asked.

"I gathered he had swum to shore. He looked kind of bedraggled." She gave an edited version of what Peter had told her, saying one of the men had appeared to try to attack the other two. Thelma didn't look as if she could handle hearing someone might have tried to kill Peter.

"There had to be more to it than that," Maryann said. "He would have called you."

"She's no dummy," Uncle Benjamin said.

Digger tried to keep her expression neutral. "The man who remained in the boat may well have caused the death of the man who drowned. The sheriff needs to sort out Peter's role. He said he swam to shore to save himself."

"Good heavens," Thelma said.

Maryann frowned. "So, if the third man stayed in the boat, why was it empty?"

"Son of a gun," Uncle Benjamin said.

"Wow," Digger said. "It's been an hour since Peter talked to me, and that never occurred to me."

"You had a rough day, too," Uncle Benjamin said.

Thelma looked hopeful. "So, maybe Peter didn't do anything wrong. Should I go down to Oakland?"

Maryann's eyebrows went up and she looked to Digger.

Digger shook her head. "We don't know everything yet, and we need to recognize that Peter hasn't been honest about everything."

"Like that he was a thief in Germany?" Uncle Benjamin asked.

Digger remembered he hadn't wanted to believe that earlier. Clearly, he had changed his mind.

"We don't know why he didn't get on his train, why he came back here. Oh, he did say to tell you he was sorry."

"About what?" Maryann asked.

"For deceiving me, I suppose." Thelma leaned into the couch and Uncle Benjamin moved to sit at its foot.

"I think…I don't know if he told specific lies, it could be more what he didn't say," Digger said.

"So, it wasn't all made up?" Thelma asked.

"I don't think so." Digger was having a hard time remembering what Thelma knew. "In addition to having the letter your brother Thaddeus wrote to Marta Durkin, Peter also seems to have what Thaddeus told her she'd find in the woodshed at her parents' home. You know, your brother said that in that letter."

Both women asked, "What was it?"

"As I understand it, a small notebook of sorts." Digger hoped Sheriff Montgomery didn't realize she knew about it. She didn't want to say she'd seen it in Peter's backpack. Especially since she hadn't been the one to go through it.

Thelma shut her eyes and Maryann stared at Digger intently. After Digger had helped solve Maryann's brother's murder, she had had suspicions about Uncle Benjamin's presence.

"Why would a notebook be relevant?" Maryann asked.

Digger hesitated. "Until we see it, if we do, we won't know what Thaddeus wanted Marta to find in that woodpile. Something Peter said made me think he had it, and it was a notebook."

Digger leaned forward and touched Thelma's knee. "It's hard to hear some of this. You're a strong woman. And you have friends."

"Okay, you picked a good time to tell her," Uncle Benjamin said.

"Where is that notebook?" Maryann asked.

"I, uh, assume it was in the backpack. I hope it didn't get wet."

DIGGER LEFT THELMA'S about four to drive slowly up the mountain toward Maple Grove. She didn't think any twenty-four-hour period had been as stressful as this one. First the tension with Franklin. Then the call from the sheriff saying they'd found Peter's passport in an empty boat on the lake.

She had thought nothing would top the call that a body had been found in the lake and the interminable time until they learned it was not Peter. But she was wrong. Hearing Peter's voice from her back seat surpassed that.

"Nuts." In the consternation over Peter's reappearance, she had forgotten about the trailer. She pulled into a scenic overlook and called Marty. "Did you go over to the motel to look at that trailer?"

"I'm there now."

"Thank heavens you remembered!"

"It could be a good story. Montgomery asked me to hang around because they couldn't have a deputy here for an hour or so. Should be soon."

"Did you give him the license number?"

"Yes, Ms. Sleuth. That's why he's sending someone. It was stolen in Frostburg about two weeks ago."

Digger stared at a bright red maple tree. "I'm surprised they didn't change the plates."

He laughed. "My guess would be that the thief figured people don't look for stolen boat trailers as hard as cars. Why risk stealing another trailer's plates?"

"Yes…but he could have switched the plates with another boat trailer. Maybe one no one seemed to be using. You know, like in the back of a driveway."

He laughed again. "I doubt these guys would get into MIT. And you have a devious mind. Kind of like Maryann."

Digger told him about the visit to Thelma's.

Marty was silent for several seconds. "She shouldn't be too sympathetic. She could get hurt even more."

"Yep. Now, here's the $64,000 question. If Robert Thorn was the third person, where is he?"

"You wouldn't expect to see him at a Taco Bell in Oakland, would you?"

"I phrased that wrong. Why was the boat empty?"

"Damn. Once we heard Peter said the other guy was aiming a shovel at him, it should have been our first question."

DIGGER LET BITSY OUT, but didn't feed him first because she wanted the dog to come back in. She watched him frolic amid the dry leaves that coated the back lawn. Her neighbors, the Gardeners, had theirs raked several times in the fall. Digger did it once, when nearly all had landed. Occasionally a few even blew into the woods at the back of her property, saving her raking time.

Bitsy looked as if he'd be a while, so she opened her laptop and tried to learn more about Robert Thorn.

Instead of just Googling his name, she added things like, criminal record, court cases, and current residence. Court records for a bankruptcy the year before came up, but all she could see was the filing information in Allegany County. That would indicate he needed money, but she had figured that.

The same burglary she'd found previously popped up, but so did one the prior year. An article in a Frostburg paper said he pled guilty to stealing a lawnmower, which he said he had stolen because he was out of work and needed to make money. The article didn't mention the lawnmower being returned.

No address came up, so she went to the White Pages site and put in his name and Cumberland, Maryland. "Whoa."

She counted the list. He'd had no fewer than nine addresses in the last seven years. Had he moved that often, or just listed different addresses on credit applications or something like that? Either way, he could be called someone of "no fixed address," as newspapers sometimes said.

CHAPTER SIXTEEN

DIGGER TOLD HERSELF that she wanted information on Thorn because it would help Thelma know more about what happened. If she didn't understand that Peter's choice of acquaintances had been terrible, Thelma could be tempted to stick up for him. Maybe even invite her great grandnephew to stay with her if he wasn't arrested.

Unless Sheriff Montgomery turned up more than Digger knew about, he might not keep Peter. He likely witnessed a murder, but if he didn't assist with it what would be the reason to hold him? Though, if they couldn't find Robert Thorn, Peter might be safer in jail than in a motel room.

Digger wasn't about to let him return to the Ancestral Sanctuary.

Uncle Benjamin's head and shoulders appeared upside down. Digger had never seen him float into the dining room from the floor above.

Digger pushed back from the table and stood. "What the… you're supposed to say you're coming!"

He righted himself. *"I'm sorry. You were so quiet I didn't know you were here."* He pointed to the chandelier above the table. *"I was coming down to sit up there. You wouldn't believe…"*

Her heart had slowed some. "That's not the point. One of these days you'll scare me into a heart attack. Then where will you be?"

"On the floor beside you, telling you to wake up."

"That's not what…never mind." She sat down again and pulled the laptop toward her. "I'm looking for information on the man Peter was with."

"The dead guy?"

"Elmo, Elmer Waterman. I don't know why I didn't look earlier." She put his name in the Internet search bar. First to pop up was his death notice, though no obituary yet. The notice gave her his full name and birth and death dates, so she entered his name and birthdate in a search.

A long list appeared, initially as a high school graduation from a small town in Allegheny County or a survivor in a grandfather's obituary. Then came the petty thefts and related arrests. A bicycle here, an expensive piece of lawn furniture there.

Then an article that could be called a human-interest story. After the death of his mother seven years ago, his crimes increased. A group of his mother's friends and a former high school teacher intervened to help him get a studio apartment in a public housing unit. The newspaper regarded this as an example of "neighbors helping neighbors."

Digger realized Elmer must have some sort of mental health issue or a severe learning disability that kept him from achieving much. Or he hadn't been around the kind of people to help him attain the most he could. He got kicked out of the apartment after he broke into the office late one night, looking for rent money that might have come in as cash.

Reading over her shoulder, Uncle Benjamin said, *"Sounds like a drug problem. He had a place to stay, why steal?"*

What had Peter said the two men called themselves in an ad they placed? The Can-Do-Man and the Make-Do-Man. No doubt which one Elmer had been.

Her phone buzzed and Digger picked it up. "Hey Marty. Did you get more on the boat trailer?"

"The sheriff's people took it. The motel wasn't sure who brought it in, but they know it hadn't been on the property for more than a day or two. About the time Thorn checked in."

"Tell 'em to compare fingerprints," Uncle Benjamin said.

"Any prints?" Digger asked.

"They brushed places around the trailer hitch, which is probably the most recent spot Thorn, or whoever, touched. They may even tell me who it was, since they think I found it first."

Digger told Marty what little she'd learned about Waterman.

"I called a reporter I know at the *Cumberland Times News*. She said the guy had been in and out of trouble, but never anything violent. She called him 'hapless,' and said he was one of those people you might figure would die young, but she couldn't say why."

"He picked the wrong friends." Uncle Benjamin said.

"I doubt he picked Robert Thorn for a friend. Thorn probably picked Waterman for a patsy," Digger said.

"I take it Benjamin is offering editorial comments," Marty said.

"Yep. Have you heard if Peter will be released?"

"I should have told you first that they took him to the hospital. He needed a couple stitches in his head and they're giving him some antibiotics because the cut got dirty. Sheriff Montgomery can hold him for a short period as a material witness."

"I hope Thelma doesn't hear that. She'll go over there."

"I stopped by her place. Sheriff was just leaving. Thelma's regaining her spirit. She told him she could go where she wanted, and he said she'd been hanging around his grandmother too long. But I think she'll stay away, for now."

Digger smiled. "Hard to believe we've only known Maryann Montgomery Stevens for a couple of years."

"I have to run. Read my piece on the paper's website." Marty hung up.

"Put it on your screen," Uncle Benjamin ordered.

She opened the *Maple Grove News* website. "Please would be good."

Body in Lake Identified
Sheriff Seeks Suspect

Martin Hofstedder, Maple Grove News reporter

Very late Sunday night, Maryland Department of Natural Resources Police received a call about a small craft on Deep Creek Lake. The caller reported seeing several people, hearing loud voices, and then the sound of a splash. When they investigated, they found an empty jon boat with a backpack hanging half in the water.

In the early hours today, Monday, Maryland DNR Police found a body floating in the lake. DNR took custody of the body and asked the Office of the Garrett County Medical Examiner and Coroner as well as the sheriff for assistance. They were able to help identify the man as Elmer Waterman of Allegany County.

The boat's other occupants were believed to be Peter Becker, a German tourist whose backpack was on the boat, and Robert Thorn, formerly of Maple Grove and now living in Allegany County. Becker was found on land, in Thayerville. Thorn's whereabouts are unknown. When last seen, he was still in the boat, wearing a wet suit with goggles around his neck.

Details surrounding Waterman's death are not clear. Becker maintains that Thorn swung a shovel, intending to strike Becker. However, he hit Waterman, knocking him unconscious and the man fell into the water. Becker has said that at that point he jumped in the lake and eventually swam to shore.

DNR Police cannot verify Becker's version of events and are skeptical of some aspects of his story because he waited hours before reaching out for assistance. At this point, since Becker was found on county land, Garrett County's Sheriff Montgomery is holding him for questioning after a head injury required Becker's treatment at a local hospital.

Montgomery said his office notified an uncle of Elmer Waterman of his death. They also contacted Thorn's sister, who lives in Maple Grove. She has not had contact with him for more than a year and asked not to be named in this article.

This story will be updated.

Digger sat back in her chair. "So, Marty found out Thorn had on a wet suit and was still in the boat when Peter swam away. Why wouldn't he have just piloted the boat back to shore?"

"Someone called DNR Police because they heard the splash. If he had a wet suit, he could have gotten to shore with a lot less noise by doing the breaststroke under water."

She regarded her uncle. "Breaststroke, huh?"

"Franklin took swimming lessons. It's quieter."

Digger studied the computer screen again. "Nothing about oxygen tanks. I wonder if they were snorkeling."

"I bet his sister has a different name, now," Uncle Benjamin said. *"Are you going to find out who she is?"*

"No," Digger said. "She may not want her brother to think she's talking about him, and all I need to know about him is to stay away." She yawned. "I'm glad Marty kept my name out of the story, and Thelma's."

"Someone's going to wonder why a German tourist was in that boat."

"Could be, but not my problem." She yawned again. "You may not need sleep, but I hardly had any last night and I'm pooped."

"What about Thelma?"

"I'm going to make myself a sandwich, call her, watch the news, and go to bed."

Uncle Benjamin's tone was plaintive. *"What should I do?"*

Digger studied him for a second. Thelma was his friend, but it wasn't as if he would be able to comfort her even if Digger drove him to her place.

"You can listen when I call her and, if it's really necessary, tell me something to say to her. We can visit her tomorrow."

"Hmph. I'm going to patrol this place all night to make sure that Thorn man doesn't try to get at you."

"What? Why would he come after me?"

"You don't know where he was when the deputies came to your Jeep. Thorn could know Peter talked to you. Maybe Thorn will want to know what Peter said."

"That's not a comforting thought."

DIGGER AWOKE AT SIX-THIRTY on Tuesday. She lay in bed for several minutes going over Monday's events and trying to convince herself that the only thing she needed to do regarding Peter Becker was check on Thelma.

She took her phone off the bedside table and texted Holly that she'd be at You Think, We Design by nine that morning. Then she looked down at Bitsy who, for a change, waited patiently for her to get out of bed. "Come on, Boy. You can water the mums."

Digger stood on the back porch in crisp morning air and watched Bitsy, but mostly thought about the last couple of days. Sheriff Montgomery had warned Thelma and her to watch out for Robert Thorn, but she doubted he would stay in the area. He'd left the boat trailer at the motel, but he had the truck or car he'd used to pull it.

Movement in the wooded area to the right of the family cemetery plot caught her eye. Further rustling preceded a fat raccoon that waddled quickly onto the lawn's edge. It drew Bitsy's attention and he ran toward it.

Digger whistled sharply. She didn't need him tangling with a rabid racoon.

Bitsy stopped quickly, as if he ran into an invisible wall. Digger waved him toward her. Tail between his legs, he started toward her, perked up when he saw a squirrel, and ran in the opposite direction.

She muttered, "Dummy," and walked into the back hallway and made for the coffee pot.

DIGGER STOPPED AT the Coffee Engine at seven-thirty and picked up a coffee for herself, tea for Thelma, and four pastries. If a light was on at Thelma's house, she would knock on the door with the treats.

Bitsy thought some of the pastries were for him, but settled for a dog biscuit.

Uncle Benjamin peered through the passenger window as they arrived. *"What are you going to say to her?"*

"Not sure, but she'll have seen the article. People may call her, because many in the senior set in town know about Peter finding Thelma. I want to tell her she can stay with us for a couple days if she doesn't want to talk to reporters or other nosy people."

Uncle Benjamin frowned. *"You don't have a gate. They could knock on your door."*

"Bitsy's bark can sound pretty scary."

He woofed and crumbs slipped from his mouth onto the floor on the passenger side of the Jeep. He gave Digger a doggy grin.

"Yeah," Uncle Benjamin said. "Really scary."

Digger parked her car and got out, balancing the two drinks. "Are you coming?"

"I didn't ride down here to sit with the dog," he said.
As she walked up the front porch steps, the door opened and Maryann Stevens peered at them. "Aren't you the early bird." She flipped the hook on the screen door and stood back.

From inside, Thelma called, "Come in Digger. We were about to call you."

Digger looked to Maryann. "Did you have a sleepover?"

Both women laughed, and Maryann said, "My grandson picked me up. I told him I could take a cab, but he insisted."

Uncle Benjamin laughed. *"I bet he did. You can kid him about being his grandmother's driver."*

Digger had no plans to do that. Instead, she placed the cups and pastry bag on the coffee table. "I'm sorry, Maryann, I didn't realize you'd be here."

She waved a hand. "We've decided to hang out for one more day."

"After that, too," Thelma added, "but more for cards or bingo."

WORK BECKONED, SO Digger stayed at her desk at You Think, We Design through lunch on Tuesday. She paused at one when Bitsy put his head on her knee and stared at her with mournful eyes. He wasn't used to being ignored that much.

"Sorry, Boy. Let's go to the little park around the corner."

He woofed and ran to a spot under the peg with his leash.

As Digger fastened his leash, Holly's quick footsteps came up the steps. "Digger," she opened the door and entered, "I just had a call from your friend Maryann. She and Thelma have been trying to reach you."

Digger felt her pocket. "I turned my ringer off an hour ago. I'll call her. How was your meeting with the insurance agent?"

"Good, I think. He's going to talk to his wife about a flyer. She's his office manager." She sat her purse on her desk. "Call Maryann. She sounded excited."

Bitsy whined and did a little dance.

"I'll take him down and be right back." Digger grabbed her phone and followed the excited dog down the stairs, fastening his leash as they got to the door. As he watered a tree, she turned her phone on and jumped as it rang.

"Hello, Thelma. What's up?"

"Maryann and I have been trying to reach you. Her grandson said they have a couple of divers who are going to look for that shovel that Peter said the Thorn man threw in the lake."

"That's great. Will he let you know what they find?"

"He'll let us sit on the shore and watch, because he has GPS coordinates for my family's property, and apparently that's near where the man drowned."

It took Digger a second to figure they wanted a ride. "When can I pick you up?"

"Any time. Do you have folding chairs?"

CHAPTER SEVENTEEN

TUESDAY AFTERNOON, DIGGER, Thelma, and Maryann sat on canvas chairs on the shore near the commercial boat rental business Digger had visited last week. They wore winter coats and scarves to combat the brisk breeze that made it feel colder than the mid-forties.

The two-person dive team sat in a Maryland Department of Natural Resources boat and donned their swim fins, facemasks, and oxygen tanks. Digger shivered at the sight.

A Garrett County deputy sheriff sat in his car in the nearby parking lot, and Digger could hear him periodically tell Sheriff Montgomery what was going on. Digger could have told him. Not much.

Montgomery had not been happy when he heard Marty would be on the scene, but the area around the small boat dock was open to the public and wasn't, itself, a crime scene. Marty had convinced the elderly man who operated the boat rentals to let him sit at the far end of his dock. Payment would be copies of photographs of the rental place and its owner.

Maryann broke the silence. "I haven't been on the lake much. I thought it would be busier."

"It's a weekday, and not high tourist season," Digger said. "Plus, people don't know the divers are looking for a possible murder weapon, so no one cares."

Two splashes announced the divers' descent. The uniformed DNR officer who remained in the boat examined something in his hand; perhaps a timer.

"I bet there's some shrinkage going on in that cold water," Maryann said.

"Shrinkage?" Thelma asked.

Digger raised her eyebrows at Maryann. "Their fingers are probably turning into prunes."

"Can my grandson get fingerprints from a shovel handle after it's been in the water?" Maryann asked.

"Marty said possibly," Digger said. "I guess finding it will buttress Peter's account, whether they get prints or not."

"It's ridiculous they won't look for anything else," Maryann said. "Maybe Thelma's family's old house is there, and they could look for," she lowered her voice, "gold coins or anything else."

Digger smiled to herself. "The house was falling apart in the early 1940s. At best there are stones from a chimney."

"I wonder if they'd bring me a stone." Thelma said. "I could put it on my fireplace mantle."

No one replied.

Digger had lost track of Uncle Benjamin, since he wasn't offering comments. She swung her gaze around the area and almost groaned aloud.

Uncle Benjamin sported a 1920s men's bathing costume, this time with a life vest. He floated a few feet beyond Marty, then came back and stood next to him, talking animatedly. Then he slapped himself on the forehead, floated out a few feet, and put a bare foot into the water as if trying to walk.

He sank like a boulder, then shot back out. Digger could hear him yelling something about, *"It damn well should have worked."* Whether he was talking about walking on water, in general, or the ghostly life vest not keeping him afloat in water, she had no idea.

Uncle Benjamin sped into the small shack that he'd checked out on their last visit.

Digger glanced at Marty's back. He had no idea of the clamor around him, and kept making rapid clicks with his camera.

She turned back to the other two women. "Would either of you like some tea from the thermos?"

"Not yet," Thelma said.

Maryann leaned forward in her chair. "There are more ripples."

One of the diver's heads broke the surface and he held up a spade with a three-foot handle. Until she saw its size, Digger had wondered why what Peter called a shovel had been on the jon boat with the three of them. Now, she realized that Thorn and Waterman probably planned to use the small spade to probe the soil at the bottom of the lake. Much easier with a tool that size with a pointed end than the long-handled, straight-edged shovel she'd envisioned.

The diver paddled awkwardly to the boat and handed the spade to the man who had stayed above the surface. Digger couldn't hear what they said, but the conversation sounded lively. She raised her small binoculars to her eyes.

The man in the boat patted the pockets of his slicker and then reached into the bottom of the boat, picked up a soft plastic lunch box, emptied it, and handed it to the diver. The man smushed it and dove back down.

"He gave the diver a plastic container, like kids take lunch in to school," Digger explained.

"That can't be for a snack, the fish would be raw," Maryann said.

Marty turned, shrugged in Digger's direction, and faced the water again. Digger felt her heart beat faster. Sheriff Montgomery said he had approximate GPS coordinates for the old farmhouse. Presumably he shared them with the DNR people. Could they have found something near the old foundation?

Several minutes later, both divers surfaced. One had the lunch bag and struggled to zip it shut. The other reached over the side of the boat and began to throw in something larger.

At first, Digger thought it was a box of some sort. Then she realized it was a suitcase, the one she'd seen Peter pulling as he went toward the train in Cumberland. If he'd had a computer in there, it would have been ruined.

"Thelma," Maryann said, "if you're rich, you're buying the next round at the Coffee Engine."

"The last thing Maryann needs is caffeine," Uncle Benjamin said.

Digger raised her eyebrows in his direction.

"I've been exploring," he said.

First one diver, then the other heaved oxygen tanks into the boat, then gripped the side of it to heave themselves up. The men almost rolled into the boat. Digger could hear their excited tones, but not what they said.

A horn beeped and she turned. The deputy stood outside his car and was trying to get the attention of the men in the boat. When they finally looked at him, the deputy put his hand to his ear in a 'call me' gesture.

The DNR officer reached into his pocket for a phone. A few seconds later, the deputy's phone rang and he answered. He listened for a moment, glanced toward Thelma, sat in his car, and closed the door.

"Now that's frustrating," Maryann said. "He'll find out something and not tell us."

Digger looked at Thelma. "If they found something that may have belonged to your family, they'll eventually tell you."

Marty had almost reached them and joked, "Maybe maritime salvage laws apply."

"Not to a sheriff who has to run for office in Garrett County," Maryann said.

THE DIVERS DIDN'T use the boat dock where Digger and friends waited. They headed north, toward McHenry, where they likely had entered the lake.

"That was anticlimactic," Thelma said.

The Garrett County patrol car's engine turned over. Marty gestured at the car as it began to roll away. The deputy waved in their direction but kept going.

"Did you see the man in the boat empty one of those soft plastic lunch boxes and give it to a diver?" Digger asked.

"I did," Marty said. "Looks as if they found something down there besides the spade and suitcase. Could have been Waterman's wallet or a flashlight those guys used the other night."

"Or gold coins," Maryann said. "Thelma, do you know what kinds your father buried?"

Digger hadn't mentioned specifics of what could be buried near the old house's foundation. Obviously, Thelma had talked about it to Maryann.

Thelma shook her head slowly. "My father only mentioned them once in my presence. My sister Therese was in the hospital for a few weeks after she had her youngest child. This was before most people had health insurance. He was fretting about not having those coins to help Therese and her husband with the hospital bill. I was young at the time and didn't associate a lack of money with hiding coins."

Maryann stood, stiffly. "I can't take this canvas chair anymore."

"Agreed," Thelma said.

Marty, clearly trying to keep impatience from his tone, gave a hand to Thelma as she stood. "Some of those older gold coins had names, maybe a reference to their design or the designer. Did you hear anything about that?"

"She won't know that. She wasn't born until 1945," Uncle Benjamin said.

Thelma stood still, thinking. "There was a saint's name, I think. St. Gabriel, maybe?"

Digger's eyes widened, but she kept her tone calm. "Would it have been St. Gaudens?"

Thelma snapped her fingers. "That's it. He mentioned that kind one day."

"What are those?" Marty asked.

"Twenty-dollar gold coins," Maryann said. "Very pretty, too."

"Are they worth much more than twenty dollars?" Thelma looked to Digger.

"If they haven't been used and aren't scratched, umm, maybe more than $1,000."

"Damn," Marty said.

Thelma sank back into her chair. For a moment she looked excited, then forlorn. "But I couldn't prove they belonged to my parents. And wouldn't they be tarnished?"

"Pure gold wouldn't be tarnished," Marty said.

"You should watch pirate movies," Maryann said. "When they open a buried chest of gold doubloons, they still sparkle."

MARTY'S TUESDAY EVENING STORY on the webpage of the *Maple Grove News* was picked up by local TV stations and the Associated Press. Digger wouldn't have known immediately, but Cameron called as she put salmon in the oven.

"So, Digger, you date Marty at the paper, don't you?" he asked.

"Have you robbed any banks lately?" she countered.

After a pause he said, "Okay, hello, Digger. I just saw a quick piece on the Pittsburgh TV station, a promo for the news. It talked about Marty's article about what got fished out of the lake this afternoon."

"Oh, yeah? I'll have to watch."

"Digger, who answered your questions about Robert Thorn last week?"

She quickly went to the dining room table to open her laptop. She didn't want to tell Cameron anything that wasn't in the article. "You know Marty and I date, and I was sitting on the shore with Thelma Zorn when the DNR officer and divers were looking for stuff."

"I don't…" she continued skimming the article, "I see Marty mentioned that Thelma's brothers and sister believed their father might have put some gold coins in tin boxes and buried them near the foundation of their now-submerged old house."

Cameron persisted. "Did you see if the divers brought up any?"

"Nope."

"Okay." He paused. "Tell Thelma that if there are any, she should push to get them. They could be valuable. She shouldn't let anyone try to buy them from her if she gets them. She should put the coins in a safe deposit box right away."

"That's quite a speech," Digger said.

"I'm serious. I put in her new dishwasher a few weeks ago. She's still with it. Mostly. But she's alone, and unless she's talking about local history, she's kind of…tentative. Somebody could try to stiff her."

Digger remembered Thelma saying having the dishwasher was like having a maid. "Okay and…jeez, what am I thinking? My cousin Franklin collects coins. He knows a lot." Not that she could assume he would want to talk to her about them. But Thelma, he'd help Thelma.

"Good. So, this is why you were asking about Robert Thorn? I saw the article about him maybe knocking that guy overboard a few days ago."

"It's kind of murky," she said. "Marty's still looking into all of it."

"What about?" he began.

"Oh, my oven timer just went off. Can we talk tomorrow?" She hung up.

Marty apparently hadn't been able to get a comment from Sheriff Montgomery or a deputy, so he'd managed to find a sergeant from the Maryland DNR police who was willing to say divers had been near Thayerville, but would only say they were looking for evidence in the "possible killing of a man who had fallen out of a boat near there earlier in the week."

Thanks to his close-up lens, Marty had pictures of the officer in the boat emptying the lunch bag and handing it to the diver, and then the seemingly full bag being tossed in the boat when the divers came back up. And, of course, he was willing to speculate.

"At least he didn't put Thelma Zorn's name in the article. But people who had talked to her about Peter will probably connect him to the body in the lake and could link it to what the DNR guys found."

"And her friends won't try to see if she has any new riches, but Robert Thorn may be reading the articles, too."

Digger used the wall phone in the kitchen. She'd left a message for Sheriff Montgomery an hour earlier and hadn't heard back. Thelma had given her permission to ask, on her behalf, what the divers had brought up other than a small spade.

Deputy Sovern answered this time. "I don't think he'll talk to you, Digger. I think he figures it's like talking to a reporter. You know, since you and Marty…" his voice trailed off.

"Could you tell him I have a question on behalf of Thelma? It will only take a minute."

After six minutes had ticked off the kitchen clock, Montgomery came on the line. "Thelma can call me herself."

"Maryann offered, so I suggested I call instead."

"Fair enough. What does Thelma want to know?"

"It looked as if the divers found some things besides that spade, and we told her that they worked for DNR Police, not you."

"That's correct."

"She wonders if you would contact DNR and let them know how to get in touch with her. Did Deputy Sovern tell you it looked as if the divers asked for a container to take to the bottom so they could bring something back up?"

"Our conversations aren't for discussion, but you can tell Thelma I will let them know how to find her."

"And did your grandmother tell you about stuff that might have been buried near the old house's foundation."

"In great detail. Tell Thelma she can call me directly." He hung up.

AS THEY ATE DINNER, Digger managed to convince Marty that they could bring a guest bed into the dining room. Thelma would be safer at the Ancestral Sanctuary than at her bungalow, alone. And the half-bath was steps away from the dining room.

"I see your point," he said. "And you did finally get those doorbell cameras."

"So, you'll help me carry a bed downstairs and set her up in a corner of the dining room? I want to have it done when I call her so she can't say it would be too much trouble."

He put his fork down and leaned to her. "I could even be talked into staying over and guarding the joint."

CHAPTER EIGHTEEN

THELMA DIDN'T TAKE as much convincing as Digger thought she might. "I don't mind Marty asking me questions, but a truck from a Pittsburgh TV station pulled up in front of the house."

"Did they come to your door?"

"They did. I didn't open it. I looked at them through my porch window and said 'no comment.'" She laughed lightly. "I never thought I'd say that."

"It's good you'll be here. You don't need a large suitcase, just a small bag for tonight. We can get anything else you need later." Thelma agreed and hung up.

Marty sat at the dining room table with a beer, his reward for helping move the bed.

Digger shook her head in his direction. "TV truck was already there. I'm glad we called tonight."

Marty opened his phone. "I'll ask the sheriff's people to drive by her house a couple times tonight. When we get down there, we'll have to tell her to leave the porch light on all night."

THEY ARRIVED BACK AT the Ancestral Sanctuary at nine-forty-five to find Bitsy prowling the first floor as if following a deer's scent through the back yard. Ragdoll sat on the table in front of the living room window and monitored the dog with a haughty air.

"Thelma, I know you've been here many times, but you haven't seen a bed in the dining room." Digger guided her through the living room and stood aside as Thelma took in the bed on the right side of the room with a decorative screen from the guest room separating the bed from the table and chairs.

Thelma turned to Marty and Digger and smiled her tired approval. "This is lovely. And I know where you keep the tea and mugs in the kitchen."

Marty sat her bag on the dining room table. "I'll close the door to the kitchen and we'll use the back stairs. Give you some privacy."

"Except from Ragdoll," Uncle Benjamin said. *"She goes where she wants."*

Digger gave him a surreptitious nod. To Thelma, she said, "If you're going to bed soon, I'll wait until morning to show you how the television works. We have an antenna that brings in a lot of channels."

Thelma yawned as she said she'd be in bed within twenty minutes.

Normally, Digger and Marty wouldn't have headed upstairs so early, but it had been a long day. Marty sat up in bed and scanned news websites to see if another outlet knew more than he did about Elmer Waterman's murder or Thorn's whereabouts.

"He must've left the area," Digger said. "Cumberland's bigger than Maple Grove, but even so, people would know his truck."

"He doesn't seem to have a problem with midnight acquisitions."

"As in the boat trailer," Digger said. "But someone would miss a car."

Marty shrugged. "Plenty of people like my grandparents wouldn't. They keep her old Chrysler in that unattached garage behind their place. Drive it once a month to keep it running. It'd be a great car to hotwire."

"That's not comforting." Digger stopped. Bitsy had gone to the bedroom window and now stood with his paws on the ledge, trying to put his head under the curtain to see outside.

"You know better than that." She moved to him and gently put his front paws on the floor. "It's bedtime."

Ragdoll slunk into the room.

"Does that mean your uncle's around?" Marty asked. "Nope.

He's going to hang out in Franklin's place on the third floor. Ragdoll likes to roam."

Marty patted a spot on the bed next to him. "Come on up, Cat, as long as you don't bring the old guy with you."

ON WEDNESDAY, BITSY barked once about three-thirty AM. Digger opened one eye and glanced at him on the floor by her bed. "You do not need to go out."

He moved closer to the bed and ruffed quietly.

Digger opened both eyes and became aware of red and blue lights bouncing on her window. She studied them for several seconds before realizing they were likely from a sheriff's car. She threw off the covers. "Marty. Something's going on."

Ragdoll had been on the floor and bounded onto the bed, landing on his chest.

"Oomph. Go away…what do you mean?"

"There's a sheriff's car at the Gardiner's. I'm going to check on Thelma." She stuck her feet into slippers, grabbed a robe, and hurried down the back stairs into the kitchen. She cracked the door to the dining room and heard only Thelma's gentle breathing.

A sheriff's car often preceded an ambulance if one had been called. She jogged up the steps, meeting Marty at the top. "I'm going to get dressed and go out the back door to see if the Gardiners are okay."

He yawned. "Don't you think the sheriff's people can handle it?"

"What kind of reporter are you?" She passed him and headed toward her room.

Uncle Benjamin floated down from the third floor. *"Sheriff's next door."*

"Uncle Benjamin's here," she called to Marty. To Benjamin, she said, "We saw them. I'm going over to see if one of the Gardiners called an ambulance."

The sound of a heavy vehicle coming up the driveway stopped her.

"I think they're coming to us," Marty said. He beat her to the bedroom to pull on jeans.

They went down the front staircase side by side, but Digger turned toward the dining room while Marty went to the front door to greet whatever deputy would arrive.

Digger poked her head in the dining room. Thelma's bed was near a window and directly below Digger's room. The lights could have awakened her. "Thelma?"

"What's going on?" Thelma asked.

Digger turned on a light on the buffet. "Not sure. You can stay in bed. There's a sheriff's car pulling up and one's at the Gardiners."

"I'm getting up," she said.

Digger straightened the tee shirt she had haphazardly put on, realizing it was inside out.

Marty opened the front door. "Deputy Collins. Come in."

Collins came into the foyer and shut the door behind him. "Just checking on you folks. Gardiners had a break-in."

Thelma's voice came from the door to the dining room. "Are they all right?"

Collins' eyebrows went up. "Evening Ms. Zorn. They're fine."

Digger gestured to the living room. "You want to sit down?"

Collins shook his head. "Thought I'd look in your cellar. With you if you like, but I'd rather go down by myself."

Uncle Benjamin floated through the dining room at high speed. *"I don't see anyone down there."*

Digger said, "You know the way."

Collins walked past her and Marty, through the dining room and kitchen, and opened the door to the cellar and started down.

Digger spoke quietly to Marty. "Uncle Benjamin says no one's down there."

Marty walked to the side window in the living room and glanced toward the Gardiner's. "Still a car there."

Thelma had put on a bathrobe over a long nightgown and sat in a dining room chair.

Collins' footsteps came up the stairs and he entered the kitchen. "No sign of anyone."

"I think Bitsy would have barked if anyone were there," Digger said.

Collins grinned. "Sheriff says your dog's worthless as a guard."

Marty grunted. "What happened at the Gardiner's?"

Digger glanced around. No sign of Uncle Benjamin.

Collins leaned against the kitchen counter. "They were upstairs and heard a metallic noise and then scuttling that was more than a mouse or chipmunk. Mrs. G. talked Mr. G. into calling us instead of checking himself. Someone had broken a pane in a basement window and reached in to unlatch it and slide in."

"They stayed in the cellar?" Digger asked.

He nodded. "Gardiners have a bolt on the cellar door. Can't get onto the first floor."

"Guess we're doing that," Marty said.

"Anything taken?" Digger asked.

"Canned goods. They'll check tomorrow to tell us what, but there's lots of empty spaces on their shelves. Their son had stored some camping stuff down there years ago. Maybe a sleeping bag, and definitely part of one of those metal camping meal deals. You know plate and silverware. The thief dropped the fork."

"They heard that metallic noise on the second floor?" Marty asked.

"Nah," Collins said. "She collects old milk cans. Guy, or whoever, knocked one over."

"Scary to think the person was in the house when the Gardiners were home," Digger said.

Uncle Benjamin came in the back door. *"I've been outside, scouting around. I think the burglar is at the far end of this property, but I can't go back there to look."*

"Are you going to look around outside?" Digger asked Collins.

Collins shook his head. "Walked around outside their window. Ground's been trodden some, but it's too dry for me to see a clear footprint. No one out there now. After daylight we'll look around more." He pointed to the door leading to the Ancestral Sanctuary cellar. "Maybe get a bolt tomorrow, in case a homeless person or somebody's figured out it's lonely up here."

Marty was giving Digger a questioning look.

She'd been about to ask Collins to check near the edge of the woods, but had no reason to give him to do it. Besides, he was alone. If an unarmed burglar wanted the deputy's gun, they could surprise him and take it.

Thelma's voice came from the dining room. "Jim Collins. I need to talk to you."

He lowered his voice. "I feel like I'm in English class."

Marty grinned. "Okay, Thelma." To Collins he said, "We invited Thelma to stay here a few days, until you find Thorn."

"Coming, Ms. Zorn," Collins said, and entered the dining room.

While he spoke to Thelma, Digger said, almost in a whisper, "Uncle Benjamin went outside and thought someone was at the back of the property."

In a normal tone, Marty said, "I guess we better get a bolt for the back porch door." He took one of the kitchen chairs and wedged it under the back doorknob.

WHEN DIGGER AWOKE again on Wednesday at seven AM, she heard Marty already in the shower. Still drowsy, she pulled on her robe and went down to check on Thelma. She found her sitting at the kitchen table with a mug of coffee. Uncle Benjamin sat cross-legged on the tabletop.

"Did you sleep late because Deputy Collins was here?" she asked.

Digger smiled. "Somewhat. Can I fix you something to eat?" She glanced at the still nearly full coffee pot and took a mug from a cabinet.

"She knows her way around this kitchen," Uncle Benjamin said.

Digger's eyebrows went up in his direction. He looked away.

"I knew Benjamin kept the dry cereal in the pantry. Found yours and had a bowl of corn flakes." She frowned slightly. "I had to shoo his ornery cat off the table three times. When she got down the last time, she swatted my foot."

"No claws, I hope."

"None. I didn't see the Oakland paper on your porch," Thelma said.

"I only have an online subscription. I'll open my computer and you can read it there." Digger retrieved her laptop from the dining room, sat it in front of Thelma, and leaned over to open the website.

She leaned forward to peer at the screen. "I suppose it's too early to have anything on the break-in at the Gardiner's."

Marty clambered down the back staircase. He called to them as he went out the back door. "I want to look around the cellar windows."

Uncle Benjamin floated off the table and out the door.

Thelma looked up. "When are you going to get together with that boy?"

Digger flushed. "We've been known to hold hands."

Thelma smiled and went back to the computer.

As she poured her coffee, Digger asked herself the same question. Marty made no secret of wanting something more than they had. What was holding her back? He thought she was skittish because her last relationship ended spectacularly. Maybe, but she didn't think so. She smiled slightly to herself. Ancestral lines ended if people didn't have kids.

Marty came up the back steps and entered the kitchen. "Nothing looks disturbed. Guess I'll stop by the Gardiner's on the way to work."

Digger opened the freezer and took out half of a loaf of frozen banana bread. "Give them this and tell them I'll stop by later, would you?"

Marty took it solemnly. "They probably already have a hammer."

Uncle Benjamin cackled.

"Then hit your own head with it," Digger said.

Thelma glanced at them. "I'm beginning to understand you two."

CHAPTER NINETEEN

DIGGER ARRIVED AT You Think, We Design at eight-forty-five on Wednesday, close after Holly, judging by the still-perking coffee. She started to explain about Thelma, whom she had dropped at the historical society, but Holly interrupted her.

"Grandmother Audrey just called from the historical society. Thelma told her about your morning visitor and I suppose Grandmother raced to the phone so she would tell me before you did."

"That sounds like Audrey. You should bring Thelma here or Audrey'll bring it up to everyone who walks in there today."

Digger didn't even glance at her uncle. "At least you know what your grandmother will do. Thelma and I stopped at the Gardiner's. Someone really did break into their cellar last night."

"Tell me more," Holly said.

Digger relayed the three-thirty knock on her door and what followed.

"Do you think it could have been that Thorn man who attacked Peter in the boat?" Holly asked.

"I don't know if the deputies found fingerprints. The Gardiners are pretty shook up. He asked me if they could borrow Bitsy, but Mrs. Gardiner reminded him dogs make her sneeze."

Digger picked up the phone. "I'm going to see what more the deputies found out." She called the Oakland office.

Instead of one of the deputies, the call was transferred to the sheriff. "We don't know more than we did early this morning, but that's not why I'm talking to you. I can hold Becker maybe one more day, but if I don't come up with a specific crime, he'll be released. I don't have people to babysit him in a motel." He let that hang there.

She frowned. "Are you asking me to let him stay at the Ancestral Sanctuary?"

Holly's eyebrows went up.

"I don't want him at Thelma's house," he said. "Too easy for someone to break in there, and my grandmother will hang out with them all the time. She'd have a harder time getting to your place."

"Thelma's at my place. We set her up in the dining room."

"Why the hell didn't my guys tell me that?"

"Don't know. I have questions for you."

"I keep telling you it's not tit for…"

"What did those divers find?" Digger asked.

Long pause. "I need to talk to the DNR police again, and then Thelma." He hung up.

Digger shook her head in Holly's direction. "Did you hear any of that?"

"His voice booms. Will you let Peter stay with you?"

"I don't want to. I suppose I'll let Thelma decide. Assuming it's only for long enough for him to make plane reservations home, I supposed I'd let him if she wants me to."

"If they catch Thorn, they might want him to testify in court or something," Holly said.

"Not my problem."

Holly regarded her for several seconds. "Thelma might make him your problem."

Digger shrugged in frustration. "She was just about Uncle Benjamin's best friend, so if she wants him to stay, he can. Right now, I need to let Franklin know what's going on. I could see Peter calling him to play the aggrieved foreign tourist."

DIGGER WALKED INTO THE Maple Grove Historical Society at noon to take Thelma home with her. Audrey stood on a stool reaching into the display in the large picture window and Thelma sat at the front desk with a pile of old postcards in front of her. She nodded her head toward Audrey and shrugged.

Digger considered the odds of the white-haired octogenarian landing on her hip or head. "Uh, Audrey, didn't you promise Holly you'd stay off stepstools after you dropped that gravy boat you were reaching for last Thanksgiving?"

Audrey frowned. "If you'd showed up earlier, I wouldn't have had to climb. I need you to take out that group of old school books and," she pointed to Thelma's desk, "put in that old rolling pin and baking pans. It's time to start holiday cooking."

"Surely not with those rusty things," Digger teased.

She stepped off the stool and straightened her sweater. "You're worse than your old coot uncle."

From behind Digger, Uncle Benjamin said, *"Better than being an old cow."* He zoomed past them and headed to shelves on the right, near the back.

"That's a pretty high bar," Digger said. She stood on the stool, and reached over the three-foot plywood backdrop to remove the pile of books, two at a time. In front of a math book was a ruler from the days before centimeters were on the thin wooden rulers.

"Audrey," Thelma said, "I saw an old flour sifter in the storage room. That would look good, too."

Audrey turned and headed that way. "Good idea."

Digger lowered her voice. "Hope you didn't get too much guidance about doing a job you've done for years."

"She means well. And I do tell myself that a lot." She began putting the large stack of post cards in her canvas bags. "Maryann's coming over this afternoon." She paused. "Or maybe you're supposed to pick her up. Anyway, she can help me identify some of the scenes on these postcards." Her eyes brightened. "Some are from the earliest years of the 20th century."

"Sounds fun." Digger wanted to bang her head against the wall. When did she start running a senior citizen activity center?

DIGGER SPENT PART OF Wednesday afternoon at the kitchen table working on a brochure for the Methodist Church's fall bazaar. Thelma and Maryann had headquartered themselves at the dining room table, having spread out about forty postcards and several local history books so they could identify buildings and, in a few cases, people.

About every twenty minutes, Uncle Benjamin would float into the kitchen to tell her to go to the dining room and look at a specific postcard. "Now, they're arguing about whether an old one-room schoolhouse was outside of Oakland or in Grantsville. It was in Accident."

After he nagged her several times, Digger went to the dining room. "Why don't you make a board at the historical society here, and ask people to tell you what they think about cards you don't recognize?"

They loved the idea and she got back to work on the flyer. To herself, she muttered, "I need noise-canceling headphones."

Marty had arrived a few minutes earlier and was making appropriately appreciative remarks about the cards. Uncle Benjamin sat on the kitchen table while Digger put a meatloaf in the oven. *"I thought it would be fun to have more people around, but it's frustrating that I can't jump into their conversations."*

Bitsy woofed. He wanted to get on the table next to Ragdoll. Digger leaned over to pet him. "Not going to happen." She took a treat from the jar on the counter.

From the dining room, Thelma called, "Digger, here are a few from when the dam for Deep Creek Lake was being built."

"Too bad they don't have any with Thelma's family's farmhouse chimney sticking up when they were filling the damn lake."

Digger rinsed her hands and walked into the dining room carrying a dishtowel as she dried them. Marty stood behind Maryann and raised his eyebrows, Groucho Marx style, as she came into the room. Digger grinned.

She studied the three cards Maryann had placed in front of Thelma. The earthen and rock fill dam construction initially looked almost like that of a large building. Lots of intersecting wood with concrete supports. And a lot of mud.

The brick powerhouse was in the last one, rising several hundred feet on the bank of the Youghiogheny River. "I'm glad I wasn't around when they built it," she said. "Amazing that the brick powerhouse hardly looks any different one hundred years later."

"What you can't see, of course," Marty said, "is that 7,000 feet power tunnel that takes water from the lake to the powerhouse. Pretty amazing feat for the 1920s. No pun."

Digger rolled her eyes at him and went back to the middle postcard, a more distant view. Near one edge was a group of men next to a huge wagon with trunks of trees they had felled to prepare the land for the influx of water.

"How close was your parents' house to the dam?" Maryann asked.

"On the roads today, just a few miles, I suppose," Thelma said. "Not much less as the crow flies."

A car pulled into the circle driveway in front of the house and heavy footfalls announced Sheriff Roger Montgomery.

"Is your favorite grandson coming to pick you up?" Thelma asked.

Maryann darted a look at Marty. "I told him Marty would take me."

He grinned. "How'd you get up here?"

"Doug O'Bannon drove me. Roger was too busy."

Marty headed to the foyer to let the sheriff in. Digger looked at Thelma. "Were you expecting him?"

"No, but I did tell him yesterday I'd like to know what those divers found."

Montgomery's voice carried. "I stopped by to get my grandmother and was told she'd found her way up here earlier."

Digger couldn't hear Marty's reply, but assumed it affirmed Maryann's ability to do what she wanted.

The sheriff appeared in the dining room doorway. Maryann gave him a wide smile. "Hello, Roger."

"Evening, Grandmother. The woman at the desk in your building told me I should keep better track of you."

"She beat me here." Digger gestured that he should join them at the table. "We're eating meatloaf in an hour if you want to stay."

He sat and nodded to Thelma. "No, thanks. I've talked to DNR a couple of times today,"

"What did they find?" Thelma asked.

He pulled a three-by-five card from the breast pocket of his uniform. "Well, you're lucky they'd heard scuttlebutt about what Robert Thorn and Elmer Waterman were looking for with your nephew. Or however many greats he is. About all that's left is stones from the chimneys."

Uncle Benjamin stood behind the sheriff and his eyes widened as he looked at the card.

"In pictures," Thelma said, "I saw they were made of stones, not bricks."

"True. Lots of clay soil for bricks in Maryland, but they would have disintegrated. Some of those stones have a few hundred years more for the water to whittle them away at the bottom of the lake."

"Anyway, one of the divers used the spade they found to pry loose a couple of the base stones and found four tin boxes. Not real big, but big enough." He studied the card. "They held thirty-two, twenty-dollar gold coins, a pair of sterling silver cufflinks, a small woman's ring that had a couple stones, but I don't know what type."

"Sapphires, I think," Thelma said.

"Wow," Marty said. "We, uh, looked up what those gold coins could be." When Montgomery gave him a questioning look, he added, "Thelma mentioned that one time, her father or mother had mentioned St. Gaudens gold coins."

"I didn't know how many," she said. "So, twenty dollars times thirty-two would be…"

"Not quite," Digger said, quietly. "I checked again. More like thirty-two times at least two thousand dollars each."

Thelma's mouth formed an O and then a smile.

"I've heard of a $64,000 question," Maryann said, "but that's a heck of an answer."

"Very helpful, Grandmother. Because of their location, I think you'll eventually get them, Thelma. But is there any way you can prove your father put those coins there?"

She shrugged. "I have correspondence that referred to them possibly being there."

Digger wondered how much detail was in Thad Zorn's diary, or whatever you called it. Could Thelma ask the sheriff for it?

The sheriff's tone was dubious. "Letters could help, but would you have any of your parents' bank records from those times?"

She shook her head. "My father didn't like banks. Even before 1929."

Marty spoke. "Where are the records for land transfers when the Eastern Land Corporation facilitated the property sales as the lake was planned?"

"I'm not sure," Montgomery began.

Digger snapped her fingers. "The courthouse. The county could have records about the sales."

"There are online property records," Marty offered.

Uncle Benjamin shook his head vigorously. *"You need the office of the clerk of the Circuit Court."*

"I'm not sure how much detail is online," Montgomery said.

Digger repeated what Uncle Benjamin had said. "I've done a fair bit of research in their records. The clerk's office records land deeds, mortgages, plats. Lots of records related to land transfers. Maybe something would say how Thelma's parents were paid. I could go down there tomorrow…"

Montgomery shook his head. "Needs to be my people. Don't think anyone else would try to claim the coins, but I want us to be the ones to document anything." He looked to Thelma. "Your parents were Thaddeus Zorn, Sr. and Greta, right?"

Thelma nodded. Digger thought she looked stunned by the value of the coins.

"Should be a lot easier for Thelma than having to prove a claim to a creek with gold in it during the California gold rush."

"Speaking of knowing to claim them," Marty said, "has this been discussed a lot in Oakland?"

"More than I'd like," Montgomery said. "Of course, no one can steal any coins or jewelry now. The ones uncovered so far. What the divers found is in some safe at the DNR in Annapolis. Except the spade. That's in our evidence room."

"Why Annapolis?" Maryann asked.

Montgomery stood. "It's DNR's main office, and that's a lot of cash to be in a file cabinet down here. You want a ride, Grandmother?"

She shook her head. "Meatloaf smells good."

"We can drive her," Digger said.

Montgomery nodded at her. "Give me a call in the morning."

"When will you call me?" Thelma asked.

Montgomery smiled at her. "When I find out anything, you'll be the first to know."

CHAPTER TWENTY

DIGGER DID AS Sheriff Montgomery had asked and called him Thursday morning as she sat in her car in front of the Coffee Engine. She opened with, "Did you figure out who broke into the Gardiner's house early Wednesday morning?"

"No. They wore garden gloves, or something cloth. Since Robert Thorn hasn't turned up anywhere, it could have been him, though why their house instead of one closer to town I can't figure."

Digger had given that some thought. "Maybe he thought it was mine. If he figured out it wasn't, he might have decided to steal the sleeping bag and stuff so he could keep hiding."

Montgomery stopped her. "That's not why I asked you to call. This Peter Becker did a lot of stupid things, but nothing seriously criminal. He's being released today."

Digger ducked his unasked question with one of her own. "Where will you take him?"

"He wants to see Thelma and Franklin. I guess he knows you aren't interested in talking to him, but you've got the place with the most room."

"Can't you drop him at a hotel?"

"We don't have to drop him anywhere. Just open the front door." He let that thought hang between them.

"Does he have any money?"

"He can have his passport, credit cards, and ID back. DNR gave me the backpack and some of its other contents, since we'll do a lot of the investigation into who killed Elmer Waterman. I'll keep all that."

Digger wondered if that meant Thad Zorn's notebook. She leaned back in her car's seat, frustrated. "I'll bring him to the Ancestral Sanctuary to talk to Thelma. It'll be up to her if he stays or I drop him, I don't know." She brightened. "I could drop him near the train station in Cumberland."

"Up to you. I've asked him to let me know his flight information after he makes his reservation. One less thing to think about."

"You think Robert Thorn's still in the area?"

"Be pretty stupid, but he may not have the money to go anywhere else. If you're willing to take Becker, be in Oakland about eleven-thirty. There'll be an envelope for you at the front counter in the Law Enforcement Building."

LATE THURSDAY AFTERNOON, a subdued and apologetic Peter Becker was napping in an Ancestral Sanctuary guest room and Thelma sat in Digger's kitchen, cradling a cup of tea. She had greeted Peter stiffly before he went upstairs.

"I told him we'd talk after he rested. I'm having a hard time believing the attentive young man who is my great-grandnephew wanted to steal from me. And why come all this way? He couldn't have known anything valuable was still in the lake. Or ever was." Her voice broke.

"I don't know why she'd give him the time of day."

Digger frowned at Uncle Benjamin and sat next to Thelma. "He hadn't met you. If he had, maybe he would at least have talked to you about it. Planned it with you instead of a couple of local thugs."

"It still doesn't make sense."

Digger stood and took the nine-by-twelve brown envelope from where she had placed it on the corner of the kitchen counter. She sat next to Thelma again. "Remember, we talked about that notebook or diary your brother Thad left for Marta, Peter's great-grandmother?"

"Of course." Thelma looked at the envelope and back to Digger.

"It was in a plastic bag in Peter's backpack. The sheriff made a copy of it for you." She slid it to the older woman.

Thelma sat up straighter and pulled the envelope to her. Digger stood. "Why don't you have a look at it first? I bet it will be comforting to see your brother's words."

Digger sat in the living room with her laptop, ear cocked in case Thelma called her.

She had sent Franklin an email about Peter's status, and he called a few minutes later. "How's it going, cuz?"

"Pretty quiet. Peter didn't talk much on the ride up here. He said after he rested, he'd like to talk to us, which I think includes you, at least via phone."

"How does he look?"

"Like he fell into the lake to avoid getting killed, got a gash on his head and, likely, has hardly slept these last couple days in the jail."

"Are you worried about having him there?"

"No, and it's just until he arranges to go back to Germany. Some doctor in Oakland is supposed to tell him whether it's okay to fly with stiches in his head. I can't see why not."

Franklin said nothing for a moment. "If he's still there this weekend and you'd like me to come up, let me know."

Digger noticed he didn't say he'd like to see her.

A SUBDUED PETER BECKER came downstairs soon after Marty arrived at six o'clock. Digger wondered if he'd waited for someone he might perceive to be an ally of some sort. Marty had probably seemed sympathetic to Peter when he told Peter to ask the sheriff to have someone look at the cut on his head.

Peter said hello as he came into the kitchen and Digger invited him to sit with her and Thelma at the Formica-topped table. It was crowded because Uncle Benjamin sat in his usual spot, minus Ragdoll, who sat in the corner of the room, next to Bitsy.

Marty stood at the stove warming up beef stew he had ordered from the Maple Grove Café. He greeted Peter with, "This is the extent of my cooking skills." He stayed on his feet while Peter began his apology and explanation.

"I am very sorry to have deceived all of you, especially you, Thelma. You were so good to me."

Thelma nodded. "I was surprised and angry at what you did. I had welcomed you."

He winced. "You did. That's when things became very... different than what I thought."

Marty leaned against the sink. "How about backing up some. How did you learn about Thelma, what brought you here?"

Peter nodded. "When my Grandmother Bridget died two years ago, she left her family photographs to me, as well as some letters and a small journal, kind of a diary." He tilted his head toward Thelma. "Before he left, your brother Thaddeus had left it with Great-Grandmother Marta."

He cleared his throat. Without really looking at it, Marty took a mug off the counter, put water in it and passed it to Peter.

"Thank you." He took a drink, then smiled briefly. "He made Maryland sound like an almost magical place. He loved the mountains, and after the lake came he liked to fish in it. He described his parents and Thomas and Therese. And some of Theodore, but he was very young when Thaddeus left for the War."

"I heard he spoke about coming home after the War?" Thelma said, more as a question.

Peter appeared perplexed. "Yes. With Great-Grandmother Marta. I hope the sheriff will give me back the journal. I will leave it with you."

The photocopy sat under Thelma's mug of tea, and she tapped it. "The sheriff made me a copy. My brother describes a much simpler time than even I knew growing up." She smiled lightly. "He said my mother insisted on churning butter even after they moved to town. I was born in 1945. I never saw her do that."

At her smile, Peter relaxed slightly. "That was a word I had to look up. I think it is much easier to buy butter."

"I haven't read the journal," Marty said. "What made you focus on items buried near the foundation of the old Zorn home?"

Thelma answered. "I just read it for the first time an hour ago. My brother Thomas had referred to my father's odd choice of a hiding place in some letters, but nothing as definite as what Thaddeus wrote in here."

"Sounded definite to me, too, but I couldn't make out all the handwriting," Uncle Benjamin said.

Thelma tapped the copy again. "I'm not sure Thaddeus told Thomas that he helped my father bury his tin boxes. At least, Thomas didn't sound that certain in his letters to Therese. Thaddeus is quite clear in here."

Marty turned to Peter. "So, you read about the potential of wealth in the lake and came over here?"

Peter shut his eyes for a second. "I am ashamed to say it made me think of it. I tried to find any of my great-grandfather's relatives to see if I could learn if the coins had been found. I really was interested in my ancestors and had already done the DNA test with Ancestry."

"And that's how you found Thelma?"

"Not at first." He nodded to Thelma. "At first only very distant relatives, in I think Ohio, and…"

"Therese lived there! Maybe it's her children," Thelma said.

Peter nodded. "But they were such distant cousins, I did not contact them. Then I had one of those Ancestry messages that I had a new match. You did not have much on your tree, and of course your name was not there, because you still live. But the message gave your contact information."

"I made that tree for Thelma," Uncle Benjamin said.

Digger tried to quietly glare at him. He had always said he didn't know how to work with Ancestry trees beyond looking at them.

Uncle Benjamin shrugged. *"I hate to type. Sorry."*

Digger realized Marty was finishing asking a question about how Peter found Thelma.

"He knew about her before he came, right?" Uncle Benjamin asked. Digger ignored him.

"Information on her brothers and sister were easy to find because they had passed. I found an obituary for her brother, Theodore. It said she survived and lived in Maple Grove. I only knew about Oakland, but I could see Maple Grove is close to it."

Digger tried to keep rancor from her tone. "So, you learned of the possibility of gold coins being buried, and found Thelma. Why not just write to her?"

Peter sat up straighter. "I…my parents are very angry with me. A number of years ago, I took a bracelet from a jewelry store. I did not pay for it. I was later arrested."

Thelma had her hands in her lap and did not look at Peter. "Were you young?"

Peter shrugged. "I was in college. I had little money but, of course, I should not have done something so stupid. My parents were furious. They said I would have no success in life, and they stopped paying for my college." When no one said anything, he added, "I do not blame them."

"So, you went to work?: Marty asked.

"Some, what I think you Americans call odd jobs. But I still went to school. I am almost finished."

"Why bother to steal something from the Zorn's old house?" Digger asked.

"I thought I could finish school faster if I had money. Then my parents might be proud of me again. They now speak to me, but they are ashamed of me still."

Digger had no way to know if this story was true, or whether any of the information he relayed earlier was true. His plan to come to the U.S. seemed ludicrous. Why not just keep working and studying?

Thelma spoke. "I understand why you wanted to have your parents' approval, but you risked everything. How did you even plan everything you did here?"

"Before I knew you, Aunt Thelma, I put an advert on your Craigslist saying I wanted someone near Deep Creek Lake to help me learn to dive and explore the bottom of the lake. I said I wanted to see what long-ago buildings had survived."

"Who's this Craig?" Uncle Benjamin asked.

Digger shook her head slightly. She'd explain it to him later.

"The Can Do Man had placed an advert for his services, and he saw my advert and contacted me."

Peter drew a long breath. "And then I met Thelma, all of you, and I wished I had not ever met the Can Do Man and the Make Do Man."

"Say what?" Marty asked.

Digger didn't want to listen to Peter stumble through how he worked with the two men. She quickly relayed what Peter had previously told her about Thorn and Waterman. As she finished, she looked at Thelma. "I'm angry with Peter for what he put us through, but I don't think he realized what a scoundrel Robert Thorn is. And maybe Elmer."

"They had the plan. I wanted to stop all the searching, but they thought they deserved whatever we would find." He put his head in his hands, elbows on his knees.

No one spoke, and Peter sat back up after a few seconds. "And you remember, Digger, maybe Marty, too, I said my mother was worried about me being here. I said she texted me a lot."

"I remember, too," Thelma said.

"It was this Robert Thorn. He said if I didn't help them find 'the goods' -- that's what Thorn called the coins and jewelry – they would hurt Thelma."

"This may be the biggest bunch of bilge he's ever come up with." Uncle Benjamin floated off the table and sat on the floor next to Ragdoll.

"So, you let Digger drop you at the train in Cumberland and then came back here," Marty said.

Peter shook his head. "Not this place. The man you call Thorn drove me from Cumberland to the old motel in Thayerville. He put his boat near the lake and then took his…what do you pull it with?"

"His trailer," Marty said.

"He put the trailer back at the motel and came to the boat with Elmer and…you know the rest."

No one said anything for several seconds. Marty turned back to the stove to stir the stew.

Thelma said, "Peter, are you asking to be forgiven?"

"I, yes, that would be good. Much better than good." His voice shook slightly. "I am so very sorry."

From his spot on the floor, Uncle Benjamin said, *"Sorry? He thinks he can say he's sorry and it's all better?"*

Thelma reached across the table and put a hand on Peter's. "I'm still angry, but I forgive you, Peter."

Peter grasped her hand. "I do not think I deserve this, but I thank you."

CHAPTER TWENTY-ONE

DIGGER WENT SILENTLY down the front staircase to retrieve a copy of the Friday *Maple Grove News* from the front porch. She wanted to read Marty's follow-up story on Waterman's death and Thorn's culpability.

Marty had told her the piece also indicated that Peter had been cleared of involvement in Waterman's apparent murder. Portions had appeared on the *Maple Grove News* web page, but the print edition put it all together.

She walked through the upstairs hallway and down the back staircase to the kitchen, hoping not to awaken Thelma as she read.

Mystery About Man's Death Resolved

By Marty Hofstedder

The death of Elmer Waterman, whose body was discovered early Monday morning, is now believed to have been a homicide. Robert Thorn, formerly of Maple Grove, is a primary suspect.

Divers working on behalf of DNR Police searched the lake floor near where an empty jon boat was found. They located a short spade, which Peter Becker, who had been in the boat with Waterman and Thorn, had previously said Thorn used to hit Waterman. Preliminary analysis of latent fingerprints on the spade show they are Thorn's.

Becker was initially kept for questioning in Waterman's death, but has been released by the Garrett County Sheriff. He plans to return to his home in Germany soon. Until that time, he remains with friends on Meadow Mountain, at the home of Beth Browning.

The reason the men were on the lake has become clear. They had heard stories about valuable items being under stones of the foundation of the former home of Thaddeus Zorn, Sr. and his wife, Greta, now deceased, which was submerged when Deep Creek Lake filled. The house itself is largely gone, but parts of the chimneys and flagstones surrounding them remain.

Though exploration of the old home's foundation was not initially part of the divers' work, they did examine it. They found several tin boxes that match the description of containers Thaddeus Zorn, Sr. had made in the late teens or early 1920s.

While more investigation is needed to sort out ownership of the contents of the boxes, the items correlate to coins and jewelry that belonged to the Zorn family. Their last surviving child, Thelma Zorn of Maple Grove, has several pieces of correspondence that describe some of the contents.

In addition, research done by the sheriff of Garrett County indicates that Mr. and Mrs. Zorn received a substantial sum of gold coins when the family sold their farm to the Eastern Land Corporation in 1924.

DNR Police and Sheriff Montgomery caution against members of the public looking for any more buried boxes. DNR warns that diving 25 feet would be treacherous for most people. Sheriff Roger Montgomery has said that if any plundered items are discovered in the county, thieves would be fully prosecuted.

When she finished reading the piece, Digger was more worried about Thelma's safety. The comprehensive piece would be on the website, too, so Thorn didn't have to be in the area to read it. In fact, if he'd left, it could draw him back.

"At least it doesn't give her address," Uncle Benjamin said.

"Or mine." Digger smiled to herself. Marty had used her given name of Beth. People who'd known her for years might know it was she. Others could figure it out if they worked at it.

Digger heard Thelma in the dining room and lowered her voice. "But if Thorn or some other treasure hunter looks into her at all, they'll know she volunteers at the historical society and is friends with us. Or they can do a web search and find our addresses."

"Technically, yours. I'm kind of her ad hoc Guardian Angel," Uncle Benjamin said.

Thelma came into the kitchen. "Good morning, Sleepyhead."

Digger folded the paper. "Hey, six-thirty is early in my book. Did you make toast or cereal earlier?"

"Yes." She sat at the kitchen table, forcing Uncle Benjamin to move unless he wanted her arm to rest through his knee. "I really appreciate all you've done for me, Digger, but I think today might be a good day for me to go home. Surely people have stopped paying attention to my family's long-buried house."

Digger cleared her throat and slid the paper to Thelma. "After you read this, you might want to stay a few days more."

With increasingly knitted brows, Thelma read the story as Digger poured herself a second cup of coffee. Thelma closed the page with a flourish. "I think Marty should have kept my name out of the paper!"

"One of the hardest parts of Marty's job is writing as if he didn't know the people personally. He has to think like a reporter and be even-handed."

Thelma pursed her lips and tapped a forefinger on the newspaper. "Even so…"

"If we look at the Frostburg or Cumberland papers or the Pittsburgh TV station's website, your name and your dad's tendency to bury family gold are there, too."

"But I didn't talk to them," she protested.

"I never thought of Thelma as naïve. Tell her how it works," Uncle Benjamin said.

"When they couldn't get you, they likely talked to other people. Media people believe when they hear something from two or three people that they can attest to what they call 'reliable sources.' In your case, they buttressed their suppositions with information like where your parents' farmhouse was in relation to where the boat was found on the lake."

Thelma sighed. "I suppose it's good I saw you before Marty."

Digger smiled. "My guess is the reason he didn't stay over last night is because he didn't want to see your hurt feelings."

She waved a hand. "I'm tougher than that. I'm plain outright mad at him."

"You go, Thelma." Uncle Benjamin looked at Digger. *"What are we doing today?"*

Digger laughed. "He'll probably try to charm you later. So, you'll stay, right?"

"I suppose I should. I told Maryann I'd have lunch with her at her senior condominium today."

"We'll ask Marty to bring her up here. She can scold him before you do."

"Good! But I'm making more work for you, Digger."

She shook her head. "I'll let you make lunch. It's a brisk, fall day, so tomato soup and sandwiches."

"I'd love to do that. You take a break."

"What I'll probably do is some work on the computer in the morning and rake leaves in the afternoon. I love the smell of leaves burning in the fall."

Thelma looked upward. "Have you seen Peter this morning?"

"No. You can spend time with him today or not. It's a big house."

Thelma stood and looked out the kitchen window at the leaf-strewn lawn and gray sky. "Would you bring some of Benjamin's local history books to the dining room? It will give us something to do besides stare at each other."

MARTY ARRIVED AT NOON with Maryann and sporting a troubled look on his face. Digger had just finished designing a brochure for Duds 'n Suds, one of her and Holly's favorite clients. Their Zoom call discussion had been Thelma's first observation of a video call, and Holly had been as delighted at Thelma's surprise as Digger was.

Digger greeted Maryann and, at her request, directed her to the first-floor powder room. Then she grinned at Marty. Quietly, she said, "You're in trouble."

"Did you tell her I was just doing my job?"

Digger nodded and spoke in a normal tone. "I'm going back to the kitchen to be with Thelma. You can escort Maryann."

In the kitchen, Digger took out a saucepan and two cans of tomato soup. "These are pop tops. You want me to open them?"

Thelma spoke as if she hadn't heard her. "If we could do zoom calls like that at the historical society, then some of the people who can't get out easily anymore could attend on their computers."

"You could." Digger popped open the cans. "And one of you could carry the computer around for a minute so people who haven't been there for a while could see the changes you and Audrey made to the research area."

Thelma almost snorted. "Those were Audrey's ideas. It's an excuse for her to order around Doug Bannon and that friend of yours, Cameron."

"What do you mean?" Digger asked.

"They move the furniture." Her eyebrows went up. "We should make Marty help."

He opened the swinging door between the kitchen and dining room and half bowed to Maryann as she entered. When he straightened, he told Thelma, "Whatever it is, I'll do it."

Maryann grinned, "Digger, you should record that."

Marty wiggled his eyebrows at her, and Digger felt herself blush. "I've opened cans of tomato soup and Thelma's going to make it."

Peter's voice came from the door between the kitchen and dining room. "I can help."

Marty turned. "Could be too many cooks in the kitchen. I'm going to take Bitsy for a walk down the driveway. Join us?"

Peter nodded at Thelma and let Marty pass him and walk into the living room, whistling for Bitsy.

"That was some pretty good thinking," Uncle Benjamin said. *"It'll kind of break the ice."*

LUNCHEON CONVERSATION had started out awkward, but the tone lightened after a few minutes. Marty left to go back to work after lunch. Digger felt like taking a nap more than raking leaves, but rain was predicted for that night, meaning it would be too wet to rake leaves for a few days.

She carried a large blue tarp to the back yard and spread it out a few dozen yards from the base of the back porch steps. Then she pulled the burn barrel to a nearly bare spot, away from the house.

Uncle Benjamin wore a firefighter's yellow coat, the triangular hat, and a badge that said 'chief.' *"Don't forget to put a couple buckets of water near the burn barrel."*

"You weren't this bossy before you died."

He assumed a pious pose. *"I was letting you learn on your own."*

Because it was a warm, sunny day, Digger dragged lawn chairs from where she had stored them under the back porch to a spot a couple hundred feet from the burn barrel. If Thelma, Maryann, and Peter came outside as she raked and burned, their conversations might be less awkward.

Maryann led the way down the back steps, carefully leaning on the railing and placing her cane firmly on each step. "Digger, you didn't say we'd be required to perform manual labor."

Digger called from where she stood near the burn barrel, dumping leaves from the tarp into the barrel. Flames shot out for a few seconds, then smoldered as the dry leaves quickly burned. "No offense, but I think I can work faster without you."

Peter helped Thelma to one of the lawn chairs, but then walked back into the house. He returned in two minutes with two afghans that Digger kept in a stack near the fireplace. He gave one to each of the older women to spread on their laps and took a chair next to Thelma.

Digger couldn't hear their conversation, but it sounded friendly enough. She looked around for Uncle Benjamin and saw him in the family plot, sitting on top of the large headstone he shared with Aunt Clara. "Good place for him," she muttered to herself.

She stood back from the barrel so she didn't breathe fumes but could absorb the musty yet crisp smell of dry, brown leaves going up in smoke. She glanced at the afternoon sky with its thickening clouds and wished she'd begun her work in the morning.

Uncle Benjamin's voice came from the family plot. *"You need to rake up here, around the headstones."*

Digger nodded, but kept pulling the dry leaves onto the tarp. As it filled, she caught a few words from Thelma and Maryann. It sounded as if they were reminiscing about Oakland in the 1960s or thereabouts, because a drugstore soda fountain featured prominently. They paused in their debate about its location to explain to Peter what a soda fountain was.

Digger brought the four corners of the tarp together so she could pick it up and slide leaves into the burn barrel. She sneezed as they began go from the tarp to the barrel.

Uncle Benjamin appeared at her right side. *"You wouldn't need to do a lot of work…"*

"Holy crud!" Leaves slid to the right, landing on the ground near the barrel and then one edge of the tarp dangled into the fire just long enough to get singed on a corner. "Look what you've done!"

"Uh, oh." Uncle Benjamin sped back to the family plot.

Lawn chair conversation stopped and Thelma said, loudly, "Don't scold yourself."

Maryann called, "I volunteer Peter to help you!"

Digger swore under her breath. She didn't want his help. "I can manage. Just stepped on a rock."

As she raked, Peter came toward her, a tentative smile on his lips. "I am not so good at raking, but I can help you put the leaves in the fire."

"I bet it's not good for you to bend over much. Wouldn't it make your head throb?"

He moved dry leaves around with his foot, which made a crackling sound. "It is not so bad now."

She raked more leaves onto the tarp. "Let's start with a small batch. Grab the two corners closest to you and I'll grab the other two."

He stooped rather than bend over. "So little weight." He followed Digger's lead and they tipped the leaves into the barrel. Applause came from Thelma and Maryann.

Digger dropped the tarp and did a half-bow. Peter did the same, but began to stumble forward.

She grabbed his elbow to steady him. "Back to the observation post, or you'll end up with a big bump to match your stitches."

He straightened and spoke stiffly. "I suppose you are right."

As he began to walk away, Digger said, "Peter. We all make mistakes."

He turned halfway. "My mistake was a very big one."

Digger shrugged. "More to learn from it."

He appeared puzzled for a moment.

"Ask Maryann and Thelma. They'll know what it means." She went back to raking as he walked away.

CHAPTER TWENTY-TWO

DIGGER FUMED TO HERSELF. Why had she done that? It wasn't her job to lessen Peter's guilt. She remembered the time, as a six-year-old, she had climbed onto her sister's bed to look at a new dress she had placed there. Climbed on with her cereal bowl and spilled half of it on the dress.

Anna had yelled, "Look what you did!" and their mother ran into the room, too. Both told Digger she'd been careless and Anna added that she'd have to wear an old dress to the school dance.

Digger ran to her room, shut the door, and curled up on her own bed facing the wall, trying not to cry. A few minutes later, Anna came in and sat on the edge of the bed. "Mom was able to rinse that part of the dress and she has a fan blowing on it so it'll be dry in time for the dance." She'd tugged on Digger's braid.

"I'm sorry I spilled."

"You're okay with me. Mom's not too happy you took cereal upstairs, but she'll get over it."

With those words, Digger's stomach had unclenched and she sat up and hugged her older sister.

She wasn't about to hug Peter.

Uncle Benjamin called again from the family plot. *"It won't take long. At least get the leaves around Clara's grave."* He now wore tattered blue jeans and a faded flannel shirt, something he would have worn to work in the Ancestral Sanctuary gardens.

He wouldn't stop until she raked in the plot. Digger looked at the trio and pointed to the graves. "I'm going to pull leaves away from the stones before they get soggy."

"That's good," Thelma called.

"Better you than me," Maryann said.

Digger trudged up the low rise to the now unfenced graves. Aunt Clara had been the first to be buried there in many years.

And Uncle Benjamin, of course, but he hadn't stayed. She walked under the metal arch that bore the word Browning, feeling almost foolish. She didn't have to go through the old entrance.

Uncle Benjamin stood next to the headstone bearing his and Clara's names and pointed to the leaves. *"Just rake them into a pile. You can come back later with a bag and carry them to the fire."*

Under her breath, Digger said. "Thanks for the stage direction."

Uncle Benjamin switched to a coat and tie, as he might wear at opening night of a play. Or a funeral.

He didn't say anything for about the first fifteen seconds she worked. *"I had an ulterior motive."*

"No surprise there."

"I think that break-in at the Gardiner's house was that Thorn guy, and he thought it was your place. He maybe got scared off when the police came, but if he read that article in today's paper, he'll be back."

Digger agreed, but didn't want to let on that she was worried. "You can stay on the first floor tonight and listen for anyone trying to get in. I'll make sure my cell phone is next to the bed if you come wake me up."

"Marty coming tonight?"

"As far as I know. But I wouldn't want either one of us trying to fight with someone." She paused, wanting to reassure Uncle Benjamin. "I think we're safe, but if I have to dial 9-1-1, we can go up to Franklin's apartment and lock ourselves in."

"But what about Thelma?"

Digger stopped raking. She conjured an image of Maryann's apartment in downtown Maple Grove. There would be no place for Thelma, and if Digger brought it up, Thelma would say she should go home.

"I smell rubber burning."

"Some of us use a lot of brain cells."

"Maybe you should sleep in the living room," Uncle Benjamin said. When he saw her frown, he added, *"I'd suggest Marty, but Thelma wouldn't think that proper."*

"We'll have to talk…"

Peter's voice drifted to them. "Who are you talking to? I ask for Maryann."

"And me," Thelma called. She sounded amused.

"You had this one teddy bear you talked to a lot when you were about three." Uncle Benjamin moved toward the woods, and Digger thought he was going to where Bitsy sat barking at a squirrel."

Digger gave the three a thumbs up, raked a few more leaves, and walked down the slope to retrieve her tarp. She got closer to the trio. "If you must know, I was composing a new ad for the Coffee Engine. We're trying to get them as a client."

"You have Bluetooth?" Peter asked.

Digger laughed. "Yeah, but not in my ear now. I was saying it out loud. I'll remember a lot of it for later."

"Good memory," Maryann said. "I thought maybe you found a ghost in the family plot."

"If I did, I'd toss him back in his grave. I'm going back to the plot and bring some more leaves to the burn barrel. Then how about we go in?"

Maryann drew a deep breath. "Do you know what the small of Autumnal leaves is called?"

"Autumnal?" Peter asked.

"Yes," Thelma said. "It's an adjective for Autumn."

Uncle Benjamin had returned from his quick trip to see what Bitsy was barking at. *"Leave it to a school teacher."*

Digger started and covered by asking Maryann what she meant.

"The word is rummescent. It means the smell and action of Autumnal leaves." Maryann looked very pleased with herself.

"I learned a new word," Digger said. "I'm going to bring the leaves down from the plot and then head in."

Uncle Benjamin walked next to her. He again wore the tattered jeans. *"Thelma looks comfortable with Peter again, don't you think?"*

"Well, they're family, and we forgive a lot with family. Even when they surprise us from behind."

"Sorry. I forget you can't hear me tromping through the dry leaves."

"I get it. I'm having a harder time forgiving Peter. I believe he initially found Thelma while trying to find his great-grandfather's relations, but anything after that was basically a lie. To people who were helping him."

Uncle Benjamin nodded toward Bitsy, who was wandering around the edge of the mowed lawn, near the woods. *"He's really interested in something, but I don't want to get that far away from you. If I fade in the woods you might not find me."*

Digger grinned. "Are you worried I wouldn't look?"

"Of course you would. Who else would advise you on local history?"

"Right." She placed the tarp next to the pile she'd already made and began using the rake as a broom to get leaves onto it.

"Digger!" Maryann's voice was loud, almost a scream.

Walking from the woods only a hundred yards from Thelma, Maryann, and Peter was Robert Thorn. He carried a small handgun, and used it to gesture that Digger should walk to where the other three were. He yelled, "Move it!"

Digger stood frozen for several seconds, then began to slowly stride toward the others, dragging her rake. Under her breath, she asked, "I don't suppose you could go inside and use the phone?"

Uncle Benjamin fell into step beside her. *"Keep him outside, if you can."*

Digger straightened her shoulders. Though she held the rake, it wouldn't stop a bullet. Bitsy danced around her, apparently thinking the dragged rake was part of a game.

Robert stopped a few feet from the others, and spoke to Peter as Digger joined them. "You were supposed to be dead."

"I can go with you," Peter held onto the back of his chair. "Please do not hurt Aunt Thelma or the others."

Thorn ignored the request and looked at Digger.

"What is it you want, Robert?" she asked.

"When I saw your name in the paper, I remembered you." He almost leered. "You look a lot better than the kid with braces in high school."

Digger felt chilled. "I have a couple hundred dollars hidden in the kitchen pantry."

Bitsy head-butted Digger's left knee. She didn't look at him. He sat next to her leg and looked from her to Thorn.

Thorn looked at Thelma. "I want some of those gold coins the divers found. You must have 'em."

"She doesn't," Maryann said.

"Shut up! Sure you do, Mizz Zorn. You taught me English. The story said they belonged to your family."

Thelma drew a breath. "I hope to get them. But Sheriff Montgomery said they're in a safe in Annapolis."

Thorn frowned and flushed a deep red. "That's a lie!"

"They're at the Department of Natural Resources in Annapolis," Digger said. "They do security on the lake."

Thorn swore the bluest streak Digger had ever heard.

"You can take the $200 in cash and I'll give you the code to use my bank card." Digger could feel sweat forming on her forehead. "You can get more money on your way out of town."

Thorn pointed his gun at Bitsy. "I need those coins. Tell me where they are or that dog that's been barking at me gets shot first."

Digger felt as if she couldn't breathe.

"No!" Thelma said.

Peter's face grew white.

"The neighbors would hear the shot," Digger said, trying to keep her voice firm. "You'd have to run with nothing."

Thorn's face was now red with white blotches and his expression contorted in fury. He aimed the gun at Digger. "I don't want…"

But he didn't finish. Bitsy made one leap and bit down on his hand. Hard.

Thorn yelled. His hand jerked and he pulled the trigger.

Bitsy jumped down and ran behind him, barking.

Thorn grabbed his hand and bent from the waist. "I'll kill that dog!" He straightened.

Digger raised the rake and brought it down on Thorn's bleeding hand. The gun flew a few feet in front of him. He came at Digger in two quick steps and tackled her to the ground as blood dripped from his hand.

Digger didn't have time to even raise her arms to try to shove him away. She hit the ground so hard her head bounced. She immediately felt stabbing pain in her left arm, which seemed to have hit the ground as her head did. And twisted under her back.

Uncle Benjamin yelled. *"Get the hell off her!"* He dove through Thorn and turned to do it again, but fell to the ground, shaking.

Thorn jumped off Digger. "What the hell was that?"

Through eyes blurry with pain, Digger saw Maryann try to tug Thelma toward the house.

Another shot came from behind Digger.

Thorn staggered back two steps, and looked at the large red circle forming on his stomach. He tried to walk forward, but only made it one step before he tumbled backwards.

Slowly, Digger turned her head to the right. Peter lay on the ground. She thought the shock of firing the handgun might have made him tumble.

Thelma screamed, "Peter!" and moved toward him.

At the same time, on Digger's left, Maryann yelled, "Stay down!" She raised her cane, but nearly lost her balance and grabbed the back of a lawn chair.

The ground was so cold. Digger painfully turned her head more to the left. She wanted to pull her hand from behind her back, but couldn't. She saw Robert Thorn's head thump back onto the ground. Maryann must have seen him trying to get up. Digger hoped his head hurt as much as hers did.

She rolled onto her left side and closed her eyes, trying to feel less dizzy as she tried to move her arm. She wanted to scream in pain, but shut her mouth so she didn't throw up.

She needed to keep her eyes on Thorn, so she opened them again. Not far from his head was a rotting tomato with several holes in it. It must have been carried there by a strong squirrel.

Uncle Benjamin still lay on the ground a few feet from Thorn. Weakly, he said, *"I'll be okay. Try to take your phone out of your pocket and dial 9-1-1."*

Digger tried to sit up. She watched Maryann come toward her, moving in slow motion.

Thelma's sobs reached Digger and she tried again to sit up. Everything spun around her and she began to fall back to the hard ground.

CHAPTER TWENTY-THREE

DIGGER WOKE UP SLOWLY. She didn't know where she was. Not next to a rotting tomato in her back yard, that was certain. She blinked.

The bright hospital room held the usual accoutrements, including a pole with a blood pressure cuff hanging from it. A small vase of yellow chrysanthemums and bright orange marigolds sat on the ledge in front of the window.

Next to them sat Franklin. "You awake?" he asked.

She took in the green cast on her left arm. "I think so. Why does my elbow hurt so much?"

"Because you fell on it after Robert Thorn tackled you. If Bitsy hadn't bitten the daylights out of him, you'd have a lot more broken." Franklin stood up and moved to her bedside. "You also have a heck of a lump on back of your head."

"Is Bitsy okay?"

"Marty took him to the Ancestral Sanctuary. There was some question about whether Animal Control in Oakland would have to keep him for a few days to be sure he doesn't have rabies, but I don't think that'll happen."

"Wait. Why are you here? It's not the weekend."

Franklin smiled and touched her right shoulder. "Actually, it is Saturday, but I've got that big case so I didn't initially plan to come up. I got called first by one of the deputies, and then about six other people while I was driving up here."

"I'm sorry."

"I'm sorry you're going to have to wear a really big arm cast for a while." He smiled. "Plus, your yard and first floor are crime scenes."

"First floor?"

Franklin's smile vanished. "Thelma and Maryann sort of walked Peter into the house."

"I saw him on the ground after he fired that shot."

Franklin's eyes narrowed. "Do you, uh, remember if he was hurt?"

Digger tried to think and found it made her head hurt more. "He was on the ground. After he fired that shot at Robert Thorn."

Franklin touched her forehead and withdrew his hand. "Before Peter retrieved the gun from the ground, it had gone off, kind of wildly. It happened when Bitsy bit Thorn. I'm afraid that first bullet hit Peter in the stomach."

"You mean, he isn't…he's dead?"

Franklin nodded, soberly. "I'm afraid so. I'm sorry."

Digger felt stunned. Dead? In her yard, when all they had been doing was burning leaves? How could that be?

"And…and Thorn?"

"Also dead."

"Are Thelma and Maryann okay?"

"Marty's been with them since I arrived here to be with you. Mostly with Thelma, since Maryann has family in the area. Holly's visited with her, too."

"This isn't…possible."

"Thelma's a strong woman," Franklin said. "Peter's mother's number was in his phone. Thelma called to tell her."

"If he hadn't looked for more family, he'd be alive," Digger said.

"That's part of it. More if he hadn't tried to take gold that wasn't his, he'd be alive."

"I suppose." She shut her eyes and opened them. "He told us we were lucky to have each other."

Franklin smiled broadly. "I think most days we would agree."

Digger thought about the last time she and Franklin had been together. She wondered if she would have seen him anytime soon if she hadn't been hurt. She tried to smile. "Did you bring any forms for me to sign?"

He patted her shoulder again. We aren't going to worry about that now. I was stupid to be concerned about it." When she looked away, he added, "They said you'd be out for a while, so I slept at the Ancestral Sanctuary last night. I picked you those flowers."

"Thanks." She started to shut her eyes, then opened them. "You mean it's tomorrow?"

"Yep. It's almost ten AM on Saturday."

"Oh, right. You said Saturday."

You had general anesthesia while they put a couple pins in your arm above the elbow. Plus, a lot of pain meds, starting with when the ambulance got to the Ancestral Sanctuary."

"I don't remember…Wait. Where is Uncle Benjamin?"

Franklin shrugged. It wasn't a dismissive gesture, but close. "Marty has been to the house and announced what's going on. He can't tell if Dad hears him, but wouldn't he?"

Digger's last memory of Uncle Benjamin was lying on the ground, conscious, but worn out by diving through Thorn. He was able to be at the Ancestral Sanctuary without her. Surely, he'd be okay. He had to be.

"I think, I think I might need to sleep."

"Sure, now that I've seen you awake, I need to go back to DC for a day or two. That big case I mentioned. Is that okay?"

Digger closed her eyes. "Mmmm."

WHEN SHE AWOKE AGAIN, Digger felt more alert. Marty was asleep in a chair near her bed, but the snoring that had awakened her came from the foot of her bed. Uncle Benjamin lay curled at her feet. He wore green pajamas and a heavy terrycloth bathrobe.

"You're here," she said.

Marty sat up straight. "Of course I am."

Digger smiled at him. "Thanks." Her eyes traveled to the foot of the bed.

"Damn solids. That ambulance driver almost shut the door on me."

Marty followed her eyes. "Is he here?"

She nodded and winced. "It sounds as if he came in an ambulance with me." She glanced at the door, then whispered. "Are you okay? I was afraid you'd fade."

"Just very tired. I'm going to sleep in the bathroom so you two can talk." Instead of floating away, he walked very slowly.

Digger looked at Marty. "He's going to sleep in the bathroom so we can talk."

Marty shook his head. "Probably better if you don't talk a lot. For once, I don't think you were doing anything risky, but you still ended up here."

"I'm not raking leaves again for a long time."

THE NEXT MORNING, one of Montgomery's deputies came to take a statement from her. His questions gave her a bigger headache.

What did it matter, anyway? Peter, a troubled soul who wasn't a bad person, was dead.

A person like Robert Thorn sowed ill seeds seemingly all his life, and had caused Peter's death.

None of it made sense. What a waste.

Uncle Benjamin cleared his throat quietly. *"I think we're going home today."* He wore his comfortable red cardigan and a button-down shirt.

Digger shifted in her bed. "You look like yourself, how do you feel?"

"Not 100 percent, but a lot better. I'll never cuss out your dog again."

WHEN THEY ARRIVED AT the Ancestral Sanctuary, Digger found the living room boasted a burgundy recliner that had a button to move the leg rest up and down. Uncle Benjamin made a beeline for it and Ragdoll jumped into his lap.

Bitsy wagged his tail furiously, but stayed on the hearth. He seemed very uncertain what to do.

"How," she began.

"I'll explain in a minute," Marty said. "I need you to sit down."

"Where did that chair come from? That's an old-people chair."

"I resent that remark." Uncle Benjamin left the chair and floated up the chimney. His voice carried down. *"I'm going to take a nap in my son's apartment."*

Marty guided her toward it. "I'm not completely sure, but I recall hearing Holly say you could put your computer on a lap desk to do some work."

Ragdoll jumped down and started for the main staircase.

"I can go to the office." Digger sat down gingerly, hand under the sling, holding the arm with the cast.

Marty grinned. "Somehow, I don't see Benjamin driving you."

Digger leaned against the chair's back. Marty handed her the control button and took a pillow from the couch to put under her casted arm. "Too bad this thing can't fly."

With the recliner now where the stuffed chair had been, Marty sat on the couch across from it. "I wanted to be the one to bring you home, but I have to get back to the paper. Lots of loose ends to the story." He leaned over to kiss her. "Your guard dog is here. You'll be okay."

Bitsy woofed and Digger heard his nails click on the floor, coming her way.

"I know. And thank you. I bet you're the one who fed Bitsy and Ragdoll."

"Franklin at first." He looked out the window and back to her. "I wish I had a way to talk to your Uncle Benjamin when you can't. I drove out here a couple of times to update him on you, thinking he was here. I talked to the walls, I guess."

"Too bad we don't have a ghost for you to talk to. That spirit could talk to Uncle Benjamin for you."

"On that thought, I need to get back to the paper. Holly'll be here in a few minutes."

Digger frowned. "What will happen to Peter's body?"

Marty grew somber. "Not sure. I expect it's expensive to transport back to Germany. I heard his mother is flying to the U.S. to meet Thelma. Maybe she'll have him cremated."

"If only he had hadn't gotten mesmerized by the idea of some treasure in the lake. He'd be alive and Thelma would have a charming new nephew."

"Tell Benjamin to be on the lookout for Peter's ghost. This is where he died."

"Not a great thought." She blew him a kiss.

Marty left, and Digger watched the top of his car move down the driveway. She would never find a more compatible, loving partner. Certainly not one who would drive her home after she got tackled by a crazy man.

It was time to tell him what he meant to her.

The recliner jiggled as Bitsy hopped on the leg rest and started toward her.

"Watch the cast!"

He stopped, then sidled up the side of the chair and sat on her leg. Digger rubbed his head. "Thank you for saving me, Boy. What do you say we add another male to this household?"

Bitsy put his wet nose on hers and pulled back, tail wagging.

"I take it that's a yes."

THE END

ABOUT THE AUTHOR

Elaine L. Orr writes four mystery series, including the thirteen-book Jolie Gentil cozy mystery series, set at the Jersey shore. Two of her books (including *Behind the Walls* in the Jolie series) have been finalists for the Chanticleer Mystery and Mayhem Awards.

Unscheduled Murder Trip, second in the Family History Mystery Series, received an Indie B.R.A.G Medallion. Other books are in the River's Edge Series (set in rural Iowa) and the Logland Series (set in small-town Illinois).

She also writes plays and novellas. A member of Sisters in Crime, Elaine grew up in Maryland and moved to the Midwest in 1994. She enjoys meeting readers at events throughout the country.

Scan this QR code to visit my Author Page.

www.amazon.com/stores/Elaine-L.-Orr/author/B001HD0X6K

Authors always appreciate reviews. If you enjoyed *Long Held Lake Secrets*, please post a review on your favorite web site or mention it on Instagram or Facebook, Let your local bookstore or library know that you liked a book. You can also contact Elaine to see if she would be available in person or via Zoom to talk to your community or book group.

Scan this QR code to leave a review on Amazon.com

Amazon.com/review/create-review?&asin=XXXXXXXXXX

www.elaineorr.com | www.elaineorr.blogspot.com
elaineorr55@yahoo.com

OTHER BOOKS BY ELAINE L. ORR

THE FAMILY HISTORY MYSTERIES
Least Trodden Ground
The Unscheduled Murder Trip
Mountain Rails of Old
Gilded Path to Nowhere
Long Held Lake Secrets

THE JOLIE GENTIL COZY MYSTERY SERIES
Fourteen fun reads (and counting!) at the Jersey shore.

THE RIVER'S EDGE MYSTERIES
Iowa nice meets murder along the Des Moines River.

THE LOGLAND SERIES
Police procedurals with a cozy feel in central Illinois

www.elaineorr.com

Printed in Great Britain
by Amazon